THE STARVELING

Cecil Bødker

Translated from the Danish by
Michael Favala Goldman

SPUYTEN DUYVIL
NEW YORK CITY

This book is produced in conjunction with an initiative by the Danish Arts Foundation to promote modern Danish classics of outstanding literary quality.

Danish Arts Foundation

© Cecil Bødker & Gyldendal, Copenhagen 1990.
Published by agreement with Gyldendal Group Agency.;
Translation © 2020 Michael Favala Goldman
ISBN 978-1-952419-18-8 pbk | 978-1-952419-31-7 hdc.
cover painting: Laurits Andersen Ring, *Fenced-in Pastures by a Farm with a Stork's Nest on the Roof.* 1903.

Library of Congress Cataloging-in-Publication Data

Names: Bødker, Cecil, author. | Goldman, Michael Favala, translator.
Title: The starveling / Cecil Bødker ; translated from the Danish by
  Michael Favala Goldman.
Other titles: Hungerbarnet. English
Description: New York City : Spuyten Duyvil, [2020] |
Identifiers: LCCN 2020042622 | ISBN 9781952419188 (paperback) |
ISBN 9781952419317 (hardcover)
Subjects: CYAC: Orphans--Fiction. | Families--Fiction.
Classification: LCC PZ7.B635717 St 2020 | DDC [Fic]--dc23
LC record available at https://lccn.loc.gov/2020042622

I

When his father finally found a job for him as a farm-hand, it was far away in another village.

"Two miles," his father said heavily, sitting down after the long walk.

Larus cringed. His mother sighed. It wouldn't be easy for him to come home to visit, and definitely not just for an evening. But he was not going to cry; he was the eldest and he had to be the first to leave home. That's the way it was in day-laborer families.

They had hoped that this first time it could be nearby, but it wasn't going to be like that. His father had said yes. He would start on May Day.

"What kind of farmers are they?" asked his mother.

"Old," said his father. "And they have a grown son at home who's a bit off. They said they can't have him tending the cows."

"A crazy person?" his mother asked, putting her hands to her face, glancing sidelong at Larus, who stood staring with his mouth half open.

"Are you sure that's alright?" she asked carefully.

"He's just feeble-minded," said the father.

"Larus is going to sleep alone in the barn quarters."

"And where does that son sleep?"

"I don't know. Probably in the house."

"What was he like?"

"I didn't see him."

The mother stood there. "But is that a good place for our boy?" she asked hesitantly. She was worried about it. The other children sensed this right away, and they stared, just like Larus.

His father shrugged. "They need to hire someone to help, and they usually have a boy like him tending the cows."

"I just hope they don't work him too hard," continued the mother.

"I have hired him out only to tend the cows," said the father. "But that son, he can work too, they said. He just has to be set in motion, like a horse. There's nothing wrong with his body."

Larus closed his mouth.

"And the wife? Did she seem friendly?" asked his mother.

His father bobbed his head from one side to the other. "Nothing unusual," he said, "but they don't have deep pockets. It will be no frills."

"And the cows?"

"Old and scraggly. Not doing particularly well—and not many of them. It has been as dry there as it has been here."

His mother sighed. "I don't know what we're going to do come winter. Nothing to put in the pot, nothing to put on the table. What have we done to deserve this?" Her voice was bitter, and the father did not answer.

"Children die right through your fingers and there's nothing you can do," she continued.

Larus knew she was thinking about their last-born child, who died over Christmas.

"But maybe it will be a bit better for Larus now," said the father. "At least he'll be someplace where they have cows."

"Do they give decent milk?"

"I didn't ask, but they must give something—and he must be able to take a bit for himself during the course of the day."

Larus knew full well that kind of thing was seen as theft, and that he would be beaten if he were caught. He was both excited about how it would be to leave home, and scared to death at the thought of it. To be left alone with only strangers around.

As May Day approached, his mother fixed up his clothes as best as she could, making them as clean and as free of holes as possible. And his father told him to come out to the chopping shed and turn the grinding stone for him. His father stood with an old breadknife, the blade of which was broken and the handle ruined.

That will never amount to much, thought Larus, pouring water into the wood trough under the stone. But it was probably mostly just to pull him aside, so his father could admonish him to behave when he was away. In any case, they stood there at the grindstone two evenings while his father explained to him what it meant to be a farmer's helper. That he should listen carefully when he was asked to do something, and not try to get out of whatever was being said. It would certainly be easier to ask about coming home one Sunday if the farmer didn't hold any grudges against him.

"And above all never ever leave your position before it's over, no matter how homesick you might get," he said.

The broken knife blade was sharpened, even narrower than it had been already. It looked a bit queer at the end of the large worn handle, but Larus didn't take much notice of it, as his father told him about how it was back when he went off to work for the first time and all the mistakes he made, and how homesick he was. And about how hard the work had been, and how hungry he always was.

"I'll take you there," he said, "and I'll try to come by once in a while on Sundays."

Larus brightened up.

"It's too far for you to go alone," said his father. "Some places there's barely a path, other places there are so many paths crossing each other that you really have to know your way. It's easy to get lost."

Larus nodded and his father laid his hand gently on the back of his neck as they went into the house together. His father set the knife down on the dusty windowsill.

They were up early the day Larus had to leave. He put on his best clothes and had his regular clothes rolled unto a bundle. And he needed some food of course, a bit of cold porridge wrapped in cheesecloth to eat on the way when they passed a brook or a spring. Then they wouldn't be too starving when they arrived.

Larus tried to pay attention the whole time they were walking, turning around to see how it looked going the other way, but it was all so uniform it was hard to remember. His father didn't say much and there was nowhere they could walk side by side—just single file, sometimes Larus first, sometimes his father.

It was past noon when they arrived. Before they walked through the strange village, Larus's father stopped and took a good look at Larus, to see if he looked presentable.

"I have something for you," he said, taking something from his pocket. It was the knife. It had a new, smaller handle which fit the little blade, which was sharp, shiny, and inside a sheath of worn leather, with a leather cord to hang around his neck.

Larus looked up with tears in his eyes. He didn't know what to say. "Thank you," he whispered.

"Keep it under your shirt," said his father. "Don't show anyone you have a knife—you never know what can happen when you're tending cows all by yourself."

Larus nodded and held the knife carefully.

"And be careful. It's sharp," said his father as he hung it around the boy's neck. "Keep it down there, out of sight."

Larus did as he was told. The knife felt strange but also nice against his skin. He stood up straighter. Now he would never be completely alone.

The farmer was standing at the gate to the farm when they turned off the village road. It was hard to tell if he was watching the road or just having a quick pipe of tobacco. He didn't move until they approached him. Then he stepped toward them and reached out his hand, first to the father and then to Larus.

"So this is the boy.—Dear me, is he that little? I thought you said he was eleven."

Larus looked down and thought that it was already starting, the part about not being good enough.

"Well, he is eleven," answered his father.

They followed the man into the kitchen, where the farmer's wife asked if they would like a few potatoes, even though she and her husband had already eaten. It had been a long walk.

Larus was famished.

"Much appreciated," said his father, seating himself at the farthest end of the table with Larus next to him.

And there were even meatballs. One large well-done meatball each—and drippings to dip it in. Larus was careful not to stuff himself, as his father had told him. He didn't want their new acquaintances to think they didn't get proper food at home. He couldn't remember the last time he had eaten a meatball. He picked it up on his fork and nibbled at it, enjoying every bite, the farmer's wife eyeing him the whole time.

Afterwards they went out to the barn where the cows were standing. There weren't very many, and Lars hoped they would be calm and friendly. He walked from one to the next, talking to them inside his head. He didn't have the nerve to speak to them out loud yet. There was a door leading directly from the barn into the room he would sleep in. It was small and furnished with just a bed frame and a chair.

"You'll have to fill hay in the frame yourself," said the farmer, nodding towards the empty cavity.

"Okay," answered Larus.

Since there was no more to see, his father said it was time for him to get going. Larus hadn't expected him to leave so soon, and he felt something inside him collapse. He felt the impulse to latch onto his father and scream that he wanted to go home too, that he didn't want to stay there alone.

His father gave him a stern look, and Larus knew that he should not cry. But his chest was hurting, right there where the knife lay against his skin, and he closed his hand around it through his clothes, squeezing until his knuckles went white. Then his father shook his hand and admonished him to do what he was told so as not to bring shame on their family.

Larus looked down at the ground and nodded.

His father walked quickly out the gate and turned down the street and was gone, while Larus stood behind with the strange man who was now his master and whom he had to obey. Larus waited. He didn't dare ask about anything. He just stood there.

Eventually the man pointed at the door to the hay barn with his cane and said that he could get some hay from in there for his bed.

Larus galloped off lightly, determined to do his best, but just as he disappeared into the barn, he heard Mistress step out the kitchen door and fill the barnyard with her voice.

"Tell him to bring in kindling," she yelled. "The woodbox is completely empty."

Master grunted grudgingly. He tended to be rather taciturn. Larus felt like he had better hurry so he didn't arouse Mistress's anger on his very first day.

Inside the barn he plunged his arms down into the pile of threshed hay and picked up such a huge pile he had to push open the door with his back to get out again. The he ran across the barnyard and in through the cow barn to the little room where he was going to sleep.

He dumped the straw down into the bed frame. It wasn't nearly enough. It was a large bed, made for two adult farmhands—and here he was going to lie all alone.

Larus had never slept alone before. At home four of them slept on the sleeping bench, two at each end. It must really be something to have a whole bed to oneself.

He ran to get more. But it was still only partially full. When he stepped back out into the courtyard, Master was standing there, still in the same spot.

"You dropped some," he said, displeased, pointing with his cane at the stems Larus had dropped while running across the farm. "We have no use for a waster."

Larus dutifully picked up the pieces.

"Throw them in the bed," said Master.

"But I'm not done yet," said Larus.

"You have plenty in there now," replied Master in a tone which did not invite discussion.

Larus didn't respond, even though he thought there was still not enough. Evidently they were stingy here on the farm.

"She needs kindling brought in," continued Master. "There is a basket in the chopping shed." He pointed to a door next to the horse barn.

Larus went running off again, and tried picking up the wood with a fork which was too big and too heavy, and it didn't work at all. So he put the fork aside and used his hands. The basket was also unmanageably large, banging against his shins the whole way. And the wood box was also enormous, gaping at him through its open lid like an empty maw.

Larus emptied the contents of the basket over the edge and looked at Mistress to see if that was good enough.

"What are you looking at?" she asked from the stove. "It has to be filled up. You understand that much."

Larus didn't say anything. He went back out to get so much wood it made him groan.

"When it's full you can have a piece of bread," she said, while she made coffee for herself and Master, and sliced the wheat bread.

When Larus was finished, on the counter there lay a

thick slice of rye bread for him with a layer of fat on it. He went outside and drank water at the well, wondering about the adult son his father had mentioned. Where was he? Just then Master came out from between the buildings from the fields behind. Larus thought that the son was probably out working in the fields.

"Don't just stand there moping," said Master as he walked past. "Take the egg basket from the scullery and go out to the chicken coop and gather the eggs. Then you can come over to the barn and help."

Larus did as he was told. He figured out where the chicken coop was by chasing around some chickens that were walking behind the buildings until they raced in to their accustomed refuge. The chicken coop was dark and spacious. There was no light except what came from the low door, and that wasn't very much, since there were overhanging trees all around.

The roosting boxes were along the wall, and there were a lot of them. Larus moved carefully down the row, feeling around in the pressed straw. There had to be an awful lot of chickens, or perhaps the eggs hadn't been collected for several days. He carefully laid them in the basket. At one place he stuck his hand underneath a brooding hen that pecked at him, and at another spot he stepped on an egg that was lying on the floor. He dried his toes off in the filth of the floor and hoped no one would notice.

When he came outside with the filled basket, he saw the son come shuffling by, a large, heavy set man, a bit stooped over. The man's arms, which were covered in mud all the way up to his armpits, hung at his sides, brown and wet. Larus stopped in his tracks, paralyzed. Even if he never heard about a man who wasn't right in the head, he would have noticed immediately that this man was not like other people. The man's face was large and blank; everything on him was large—his beard, his hair, his body. His shoulders and arms were enormous, but he walked like he was sleepwalking. His hands were big as shovels and they hung curled and loose at the ends of his arms. The sight of him made Larus afraid. Anything that man squeezed with his hands would be crushed.

Larus hurried in with the eggs and then back to the barn as he had been told. Master was inside and told him to clean out between the cows, and to scrape all the manure and bedding into the manure trough. Larus didn't give any sign of what he had seen. He just scraped the floor. At the same time he kept an eye on the courtyard, and he saw the son approaching the barn door. Larus was glad Master was there walking in the feed aisle, forking up hay to the animals, so he wasn't alone.

No one spoke. The large man ducked inside and walked right over to the wheelbarrow with the broad manure fork, and he started shoveling the manure up into the wheelbarrow. His gaze scanned past Larus without regard, almost as if he hadn't seen him. Maybe he was used to there being a farm boy around and he couldn't tell the difference. A boy was a boy.

Larus kept scraping the floor as he thought about the next day, when we was going to go out in the surrounding terrain with seven cows he didn't know and who didn't know him. He got butterflies in his stomach thinking about it, and he carefully laid a hand on each cow as he worked the scraper underneath its belly. In the last stall there was a large pile of hay with a longish depression in the middle.

So that's where he stays, Larus realized with a shiver. This is where the son slept—not far at all from the room where he himself was going to be. There were no bedclothes, not a comforter nor a pillow, not even a blanket; but on the side of the stall hung a horse blanket. Did he sleep with that over him? Like a horse or a sick cow? Larus looked sidelong at the stall.

At least the son had a healthy pile of straw, which rose op high on both sides of the depression. Larus compared it to the meager pile he was going to sleep on and felt disheartened. Were they going to give him a comforter, or just an old cloth?

Then Mistress came out to milk, and the son went and sat in his pile of straw. She had brought food out for him too, in a large clay dish with a lot in it. It was obvious the son was excited to get this, from his movements and little sounds he made, which weren't real words, but more like what toddlers would say, though in a grown man's voice. The strangeness of it all made Larus freeze on the spot.

"What are you staring at?" snapped Mistress. "If you're finished working, go to your room. I put a comforter in there for you."

Larus slipped into his room without a peep.

"I'll come and get you in a little while. You have to learn how to milk," she said as he was closing the door.

As he stood there on the uneven floor he couldn't help but overhear her talking to her son, coaxing him and babbling with him, like people do with chickens or puppies or infants. And even though Larus didn't want to see it, his eyes had shown him what was in the dish. It looked like something for a dog. It was a pile of cold porridge scraped out of a pot and piled up in large clumps, along with cold potatoes and various chunks of bread. In the other hand she had a pitcher of milk.

She called him Hartad.

It sounded like a name from the bible. When the priest read his sermon there were always a lot of strange names: Peleg, Jehovah, Bileam, and things like that. So it could be from that. It seemed so strange that Hartad couldn't speak but he could shovel manure.

Then Larus caught eye of the comforter hanging over the edge of the bed frame. He didn't notice it when he first came in, because everything he had seen in the barn had completely filled up his head and his eyes. But now he saw it. A large coarse comforter of thick woolen fabric stuffed with large feathers. It was brown and stained, but he was glad to have it, so he wouldn't have to lie there with nothing or with a horse blanket over him. At home they didn't always have a sheet either; but lying right on the straw was something a person got used to. What worried him was the thin layer of straw and the cold that would come up from the stone floor underneath. He gathered the straw together at one end of the frame and felt it. Why should he have such a little bit when Hartad out there had so much?

He was startled when Mistress suddenly opened the door to his room and told him to come out.

"Don't just stand there looking miserable," she snapped. "Come out and help me."

Larus had never milked before. His mother helped in the barn on one of the farms in their village, and when he was younger he used to go with her. So he knew how it looked and how it sounded, but he had never done it himself.

Mistress sat down by the first cow and leaned her scarved head against its side. After placing the wooden pail beneath the udder, she put her hands on two of the teats and explained to him what she was doing with her fingers.

"Now you do it," she said, standing up.

Larus slid onto the stool and got himself in position with his tousled bangs against the cow's warm hide. He grabbed the teats; it didn't look so difficult.

Just then the cow kicked at him, knocking over the pail and spilling whatever milk was inside.

Mistress's face went taut and Larus's ears were burning, but she didn't say anything and she didn't hit him on the back as he had expected.

"Try again," she said, after he had picked up the pail. "But be more gentle." Then she stood by the cow's head and scratched it between its horns and on its neck while speaking gently to it. The cow stretched its head with pleasure, inviting more petting. It must have forgotten that a stranger was touching it, because it didn't do anything.

Larus was pulling and sweating and trying to remember everything the woman had explained, but no milk was coming out.

"Easy, easy," murmured Mistress, who stood there letting him fumble through it.

Larus was just about to give up, but then suddenly some milk came out—a thin hard stream that made a loud noise when it hit the bottom of the pail. It made him jump, and the cow noticed him. It kicked and knocked over the bucket again.

"Idiot," mumbled the woman. "Move."

Larus got up and Mistress finished milking the cow. He stood next to her, listening for Hartad, who was rummaging around in his straw cave, muttering to himself. It sounded like he was in a good mood.

"You can try again tomorrow," said Mistress as she stood up and moved to the next cow.

Larus walked down the feeding aisle, talking to the cows, but it was cut short. There were only three cows to milk, and as soon as Mistress had left with the pail, Master came and told him to climb up through an opening in the ceiling and throw down straw for bedding. Larus clambered up the ladder and started tossing down straw with a fork that was up there. The straw was old and gave off clouds of dust. Larus understood why she wanted to have the milk in the kitchen before the straw was sent down. Larus went as fast as he could, thinking that if he threw down more than was needed, he could probably take some for his bed. Better to have dusty straw than no straw.

"Stop, stop—no more, boy! What are you thinking?" he yelled from below.

"What?" yelled Larus, sticking his head down through the hole.

"What the devil has gotten into you?" hissed Master. "How much straw were you planning to spread under seven measly cows?"

Larus brought the fork down with him and began separating the straw into seven piles. He didn't think there was too much, not at all. But Master was stingy with it because he didn't have enough. He was still stewing over last year's poor growth, and if the drought this spring kept up, the same thing could happen again. Still the boy stole a bit from each cow after Master left, and he put it in his bed. Just as he finished, Mistress came and said it was time for supper. Before she left she laid the blanket over Hartad, who had already fallen asleep.

Inside the kitchen stood a dish of cold potatoes from lunch and a board with slices of bread spread with fat. In front of Larus's place was a cup of milk, while the couple drank something that looked like beer.

Right after supper the man said goodnight and disappeared through a door, so Larus was left alone with Mistress. He was tired, very tired, but he wanted to be good, so he asked if he should help her clear the table and wash up.

She turned to him angrily.

"I can take care of my own kitchen," she said. "You won't get anything by doing extra. You get what you get."

Larus bowed his head; his cheeks were red. That wasn't why he had asked, but he didn't dare say anything.

"Thanks for the meal," he murmured instead, getting up from the bench. "And good night." He walked across the barnyard to his room, and crawled underneath the heavy comforter.

II

Mistress woke him and remained with him for morning milking in the barn. Larus glanced at the pile of straw with the big depression, but it was empty. The horse blanket was hanging in its spot over the stall frame.

Master had probably taken him out to dig peat or to the ditch he was working on—or whatever else he did. Larus remembered that his father had said he had to be set in motion like a horse—the only thing he evidently could do on his own was to walk home, also just like a horse.

When Larus later had been in the kitchen and eaten porridge with milk, and had eaten it all up, and had been given a hunk of half-dried rye bread in a little towel to take with him, Mistress walked with him to the barn to let the cows out and see them off.

"Where do you want me to take them?" asked the boy amid the noise from the rattling chains.

"You'll figure it out. You just have to walk behind them out of town and keep going until there aren't any more farm fields. Then keep an eye on them so they don't walk on anyone's newly sown ground. Master will hit you if they make trouble."

Larus swallowed heavily and looked sheepish.

"Oh, you little runt," she sighed. "Do you have a stick?"

"No," said Larus, feeling the knife through his shirt. But he could cut one, he thought.

"You won't be able to keep them out of the fields unless you have something to give them a good whack. They figure that out real quick. They're good cows and easy going—but they're hungry too. Don't open the door yet."

Mistress disappeared out the other side of the barn and came right back with a hefty branch from the rear hedge—with side branches and twigs and everything on it. The branch was just starting to leaf out.

"Here," she said, handing him the branch which was much too large. "And here," she said, taking from her apron pocket two wrinkled apples from the previous fall. "Use these to lure the cows away if you get into trouble, but don't go and eat them yourself; you can use them again tomorrow."

Then she opened the door to the courtyard, and the cows rushed out, continuing through the gate to the village road. Larus hurried after them with the branch over his shoulder and Mistress on his heels. She wanted to see how things were going to proceed.

The cows turned to the one side on their own, and Larus thought it must have been the right way, since she didn't say anything. He wondered if she would mind if he broke off some of the side branches. The entire branch was too heavy for him; he couldn't swing it to hit anything, not even with two hands.

"Hurry up," she yelled after him, as he was lagging behind the animals.

Larus ran. The branch bumped up and down painfully on his shoulder. Darned woman, he thought angrily. Why should he be carrying around a whole tree? He couldn't run with that.

Larus knew he was a good runner; even though he was small, he was fast. But he couldn't get up any speed carrying this giant branch. He started pulling at the side branches as he made his way, but he wasn't strong enough to tear them off.

The knife, he thought. The knife. But not right now. He couldn't take his eye off the lead cow.

Larus swung the branch down from his shoulder and dragged it behind him, hissing in the gravel, and the cows' ears turned back to listen. Maybe the sound will keep them moving—he was just about to believe that. But then things went bad. At the very last field the cows turned without warning onto a field of short green rye and started grazing.

After them, get them! Larus jumped like a madman, trying to hit them with the unmanageable branch, yelling and screaming, but there was nothing behind the blows. The cows paid no attention. They just ate.

So he pulled an apple out of his pocket and stuck it underneath the lead cow's muzzle. Then he knelt down in the rye and pressed the apple right up to its nostril.

It didn't do a thing.

Then he bit into the apple until juice came out of it and he tried again. The cow sniffed at it and Larus stood up quickly. The cow lifted its head and followed the apple as the boy slowly began walking backwards, carefully, carefully back towards the road. If only no one saw it, dear God, if only no one saw it.

The cow followed him, but none of the others seemed to notice. Larus started to wonder if he had chosen the right cow. But he kept walking backwards, coaxing it, and then all at once the others turned and followed. Larus felt a rush of relief, even as he saw with dismay how dry earth and green shoots had been littered around by their hooves.

The field looked messy where they had been.

When he was walking on the road with the cows again he realized that he had put down the branch when he took out the apple, and it was lying far inside the field, and he couldn't get it back. He would have to run ahead with the apple as fast as he could to get them away from that dangerous place. In this dry spring, rye was about the only green around, so it was very tempting.

Farther out lay a half-parched grassland sprinkled with trees; small patches of woods with open land in be-tween. But there was nothing that would really fill a cow's belly. He figured he was in safe territory, so he looked around for a hazelnut bush and cut off a nice big switch, one he could actually use. With that in his hand he felt better.

Later he found a half-dried creek bed with some green on its banks, where the cows could drink and eat whatev-er was there. Here he rested, ate his chunk of bread, and drank from the water too, like a dog, with his face down at the water surface. This was the best place he had seen that day, and he stayed there nearly until sundown, when the cows began to walk home all on their own. And it was good that they knew the way, because Larus wasn't so sure himself, and he could just follow them.

Larus was tired by the time they made it back to the village, and if not for that rye field, he would have been content. He just hoped that no one noticed.

But as soon as he entered the paving stones of the farm he noticed another man, a stranger standing beside Master outside the barn waiting—and what's more, the stranger held in his hand the branch he had dropped. Larus recognized it right away.

The two men waited until he had put the cows in their stalls and tied them, then Master stuck his head in the door and yelled, "Come out here for a minute."

Larus obeyed, though his heart was pounding. He knew what it was about, and in his bare feet he slowly approached the two men. His eyes were afraid and open, and he didn't dare look up.

"You let the cows go on Mads Peter's field," bellowed Master.

Larus stared at his feet. "They ran away from me," whispered Larus.

"There's no such thing," replied Master.

Larus cringed. "No," he whispered.

"Do you know what something like that costs?" "Yes." Larus didn't move.

Master grabbed him by the neck and bent him over his knee, where he hung without touching the ground. Larus's heart pounded against Master's thigh.

"You can hit him. Give him what he deserves," said Master to Mads Peter.

Mads Peter hesitated. Larus awaited the blows.

"Use that branch," said Master. "Give him what for."

Mads Peter still hesitated. "I don't know," he mumbled. "You've got yourself no more than a baby this time. How can you hit that? What do you want with a little kid like that?"

"His father told me he was eleven when he made the contract." Master put Larus back down, but he didn't let go of him.

"You hear that Mads Peter is so nice to let you off the punishment," he said. "But God help you if this happens again."

"Yes," whispered Larus, and Master let him go. His legs were quivering beneath him as he ran as fast as he could to the safety of the barn. It made no sense. Why didn't they beat him? It was his fault the cows had damaged the field and eaten some of the grain. It took him a long time to calm down again.

"He looks like one who never had enough to eat," said Mads Peter outside.

"I'm sure there's some truth to that," said Master. "The father didn't have much meat on him either, but still they keep having a new baby every year." The two men walked away in conversation towards the gate, and then Mistress came into the barn with the wooden pail, to watch Larus milk one of the cows.

The next morning Larus slipped a length of rope around the neck of the lead cow and walked beside it holding the other end. Not that he thought he could hold it back if it really wanted to do something, but then at least he would notice it right away so he could take out the apple and put it under its nose.

When they neared the field of rye, Larus patted the cow on its neck and talked gently to it and promised it all the most delicious things if only it wouldn't turn onto the field. He was sweating with worry. But the cow stayed on the road with all the others behind it, as if they were only thinking about the place by the stream where they had been the previous day.

Larus was grateful.

Time passed and the days were much the same, the only difference was that he had to walk farther and farther to find good areas for the cows to graze. The grass was yellowed and stunted, and the sky was dry as if rain would never fall again. But the trees still leafed out, and Larus climbed up and cut off branches for the constantly hungry cows. Afterwards he made switches from the branches to swat away stable flies and horseflies when they landed on the warm animals. But one day the weather turned, and there was a period of rain that seemed like it would never stop. Larus walked around damp and exhausted; standing under a tree didn't help very much, and the wind was everywhere. But the rain made the grass grow, and the cows started giving more milk. Now he dared to milk a small amount for himself in the middle of the day, into a broken cup he had found in the chicken yard. He dipped his bread into it.

But he was cold. He had nothing to put on as protection; his clothes didn't even dry out from one day to the next. This made him look longingly at an old fox hole in the side of a hill. Just over the entrance to it, the roots of a large tree curved around like talons from a giant eagle. In front of the hole was a flattened pile of dirt and gravel. The fox didn't live there anymore, he was sure of that; there was no trace of it.

What if he made the hole a bit bigger? He took his cup and started digging, while keeping an eye on the cows at the same time. He scraped the sides of the hole and tossed the dirt outside with his hands. It wasn't until several days of this that he was able to bring his legs inside too. He wasn't as cold, since he had something to do. He kept at it until he had created a rounded cave where he could sit protected from the weather, and it was so small that it got warm from his body heat. He kept his cup there, and he put his hard hunk of bread there when he arrived in the morning. And he sat there while he ate it.

Which is what he was doing the day a girl stood at the bottom of the hill looking up at him. Larus stopped chewing, with the cup in his hand.

Where did she come from? He hadn't heard or seen anything. She just appeared there as if she had risen up out of the ground. Saliva collected around his teeth, and he chewed some more while he stared out at her.

She wasn't very big, nothing on her was big except for the eyes in her thin face, which showed all her bones. But her eyes were much too big, and set deep in their sockets. And she stared the whole time at his bread which he was still holding up in front of his mouth—not at him, but at the bread, of which his teeth had nibbled off all the corners.

Larus had never seen a girl like her before, so little and skinny and incredibly dirty; and it wasn't just her clothes, it was all over—her face, her hands, and her arms and her feet, which stuck down from a ragged skirt. Even her hair was filthy. The girl was a dirty grayish brown all over, except for her eyes which were bright blue. She was totally drenched, but even the rain dripping off her didn't change her color.

In the middle of staring, he asked, "Who are you?"

She didn't answer, but just kept staring at the hunk of bread as if she hadn't heard him.

Larus though that was strange. Was she real? Was she

like a ghost? But then she would have been white or nearly transparent—and able to float in the air.

"Where did you come from?" he asked. And while he waited for her to answer, he put the bread to his mouth and sucked on it. The girl didn't say a word, she just kept staring, and he saw her mouth make unconscious chewing motions. When he swallowed, so did she.

"Are you hungry?"

He had asked without thinking. There wasn't enough bread for both of them. There wasn't even enough for him.

She nodded and swallowed again.

"Here," he said, handing the hunk of bread out through the cave opening.

She struggled her way up and crouched down outside the hole. The cave wasn't big enough for two, he thought. But at least she was a person. Larus noticed the way she attacked the bread, which was softened on the outside and very hard on the inside. She's eating like a hungry dog, he thought.

"Do you want a cup of milk?" he asked.

She looked at him like she didn't understand what he said.

"Milk?" he repeated.

It was like she was deaf, he thought, and he crept out of the hole and slid down the slope with his cup. He milked a bit from a different cow than the one he had taken from for himself.

She stood there outside the cave with the bread in her mouth when he came back up, and there was a smell coming from her that he didn't recognize. Maybe it was all that dirt on her, but he didn't say anything. The girl drank down the milk all at once and gave him back the cup as if she wanted more, but he didn't dare milk any more. Mistress would notice. He left the cup in the cave, thinking that he would clean it out with dirt and grass in a ditch before using it himself again. He didn't like that smell. He had to move away from her.

"Try sitting down in there," he said, standing outside the cave, watching how she softened the bread with her saliva.

"Have you never had milk before?" he asked, to find out more about her.

She moved her lips as if she wanted to say something. He waited.

Very slowly she said, "I don't know."

Larus thought the way she talked sounded strange.

"Where are you from?" he asked. If she had answered "Up out of the ground," he would have believed her. But she didn't answer.

"Do you have a name?"

"Tinka."

Larus turned so he could keep an eye on the cows and keep talking to her at the same time. But she didn't answer most of his questions, or she said she didn't know. "I don't know," she said, in this strange way, as if she had to think very hard to find the right words. She didn't even know how old she was. And she didn't say a word when he asked where she lived, nor when he asked about her mother and father. And she kept sucking on the bread at her mouth the whole time.

"Why are you so hungry," he asked.

"I don't know."

"Don't you get bread?"

She shook her head.

"What do you get?"

"Nothing."

"Then what do you eat?"

"I don't know. Lots of things."

"What kind of things?"

"Flies and things like that."

"Flies?" Larus felt nauseous.

She nodded. "And worms and beetles and seeds—just like the chickens."

"The chickens? Do you have chickens?"

She nodded. "Two," she said.

"Why don't you eat them?"

She stared at him horrified and went silent.

Larus waited.

"Then they would be gone," she whispered.

Larus didn't reply. There was something in the way she said it—something about the horror in her eyes.

When she had gobbled down all his bread, she crept out of the little cave and down the hill and walked across the meadow to a side where he had never been. He watched her, but she didn't turn around.

"What's that smell on you?" asked Mistress when he came back.

"Nothing," said Larus, walking outside and washing up at the water trough. He didn't dare say anything about the girl.

The following day she was sitting in the cave when he arrived.

Larus thought that might happen. The previous day

he had been famished when he got back to the farm, and Mistress had noticed it at supper.

"Are you not getting enough to eat?" she asked intently.

Larus looked down at his empty plate and didn't know what to answer.

Seeing his shyness, she said, "Would you like to have a bit more food than you're getting?"

Larus nodded.

The next morning she put a bit more bread and a few boiled potatoes in the cloth, before she tied the corners and gave it to him.

"It would be nice if you started growing," she said solemnly, eyeing him up and down.

She also gave him a little more porridge in the evenings and more milk on it too. The cows were milking better all the time—and now the ones that couldn't get pregnant before would probably be able to have calves soon; then things would be quite good.

That day it didn't rain much at all, and Larus gave Tinka a large potato and a cup of milk as soon as he arrived. He got the feeling it was almost too much all at once, that she was more used to eating a very small amount at a time. Afterwards she walked with him beside the cows and there was that smell again.

"Why don't you get washed?" he blurted out.

"Washed?"

"You're filthy all over—your head, your hands, everywhere."

Tinka looked at her hands and put them behind her back.

He asked her, "If you can't do it yourself, why doesn't your mother wash you?"

She looked down at the ground.

"Maybe you don't have a mother?" he asked a bit more cautiously.

"I do," she said. So she did have one.

"Why doesn't she make you get washed?"

Tinka didn't answer. And Larus thought they must have a strange family. His own mother was always checking all their necks and ears and throats. Proper people don't go around dirty, she always said, if she found something not to her liking.

He thought Tinka was strange.

"You can do it yourself, you know," he said, when she still didn't say anything.

She stared at him, surprised.

"In a ditch or a stream or some other water," he said.

"I can?" she asked in disbelief.

"Try it," he said, showing her the ditch where the cows drank. She stood indecisively on the bank when he looked back at her.

How could it be that she didn't know something like this? Why was everything about her so strange? The way she talked, like she couldn't find the words. He tried to compare her to Hartad, but she wasn't like that. And why did she eat flies just like the chickens, and worms? Did they have no food? Or could it be the mother was someone like Hartad? Larus thought about it but didn't get any farther.

"Do you have a father?" he asked when she came up from the ditch and her face was a shade lighter. Now it was easier to see how she really looked—but she wasn't clean. Her cheeks were hollow.

"He was buried," she said slowly and carefully.

"You mean he died?"

"Yes, he was buried, a long time ago."

"But you still live in the house? You and your mother?"

She said they did.

"What kind of a house is it?" he asked.

"Just a house."

He gave her a cup of milk and half his bread midway through the day, and he didn't milk any for himself.

When she was done eating, he pointed at her and asked, "Do you have any other clothes than what you have on?"

She looked down at herself.

"These are my clothes," she said.

"But do you have any others?"

"What others?"

"To change into."

She got this strained expression when there was something she didn't understand. Larus knew that he didn't have that many clothes himself, but he had his Sunday clothes and his regular clothes—and they were pretty dirty, but not compared to Tinka's. And then there was that smell always surrounding her.

One day he told her. She smelled her one shoulder and arm but she didn't notice anything.

"No I don't," she said. "I don't smell."

It must be because she's used to it, thought Larus. He didn't think he could ever get used to it.

"You are going to have to wash yourself some more," he said.

"But I did," she said offended.

"Proper people wash their hands and face every day," he said, wishing that she would just go away.

But she kept coming back. Every single day there she was sitting in the cave when he arrived, until finally he started going other places on some days, to get away from her. But he couldn't resist going back to see if she was still there, and each time she was sitting solemnly in the cave waiting for him. And the thought that she had to eat flies and earthworms on the days he didn't come plagued his conscience.

Larus felt trapped. On the one hand it wasn't his responsibility to take care of her—since she had a mother. On the other hand he had to give her something since she was so hungry. But it was strange that Tinka would come hang around him all day. Didn't she have to go home and help out?"

One day Larus asked, "Can I go back with you to your house?"

She looked up startled, as if he had hit her.

"Can I?" he said.

Tinka shook her head.

"Why not?" he asked. But Tinka wouldn't answer. She never talked about herself. He knew nearly nothing about her except what he could see for himself.

"I could just follow you," he said, pressuring her.

"You have to stay with the cows," she countered.

"They can come. Is it far?"

She nodded.

"You can't make it back to the village before dark," she said.

Then it was Larus who was quiet a long while.

"Maybe someday," she said noncommittally.

Someday? That could be a long time, he thought.

There were some days when it rained so hard that the two of them had to sit pressed together in the cave. Those days Mistress smelled something and wrinkled her nose.

"Why do you smell like that?" she asked.

"I don't know," he lied. He knew it was Tinka.

"Where have you been?"

"The usual place," he said.

"You smell like a sick dog," she said, "or one that rolled on a dead animal, pyew."

Larus knew he would have to do something, but what?

<h1 style="text-align:center">III</h1>

He decided to give her an ultimatum.

"Either you let me go home with you and see where you live, or you can't come out here anymore with me and the cows," said Larus. "If you don't show me where you live then I won't give you any food or milk."

Tinka looked afraid. She could hear that he meant it, and Larus was nearly regretting that he had spoken to her so sternly. But he just had to know more about who she was before he said anything to Mistress.

Tinka squirmed and didn't know what to answer, and Larus sensed that she felt trapped. Something serious was preventing her from taking him with her.

"When you say yes I'll give you some milk, and then we can walk to your mother's house, and afterwards I'll give you some bread." Larus turned and stared directly at her. Tinka squirmed with uncertainty.

"Otherwise I'll leave and never come back here again."

"Never?" Tinka took several short breaths and her hands fidgeted constantly.

"No, never again." He knew it wasn't very nice to use her hunger against her, but he had to know why she was the way she was.

Tinka looked down at the ground as if in pain. Then she made her decision and her face went taut, becoming small and angular. She looked like she did back when he met her for the first time.

"Does that mean yes?"

Tinka nodded and he gave her the milk. She drank it

slowly, as if she was stalling. Then they left. Tinka walked in front, with Larus next to the cows. He thought her little back seemed to be even smaller. Her shoulders were hunched as if she were cold, or as if she were guarding against something.

They walked for a long time. Larus paid attention to the direction of the sun and to the landscape, to be able to find his way back. But as they approached a dense growth of trees, the cows stopped and turned their heads. They wouldn't go any farther.

"Is it here?" Larus looked around. There weren't any houses.

Tinka nodded. Her arms hung by her sides in a strange defenseless way; she was still afraid.

"Can they stay here?" he asked.

"Sure," she said, shrugging her shoulders.

Larus patted the cows' necks.

"Are you sure you want to come?" asked Tinka flatly.

Larus had butterflies in his belly, but after what he had said to her that morning he had to keep going. He didn't want to, but he followed her.

In among the trees lay a couple of run-down shacks. One to live in and one for a shed. They were both made of wood and peat, with sunken roofs, and decayed by wind and weather.

Tinka walked first towards the one, which Larus figured was a shed. The door was ajar and the two chickens they had talked about came running out when they heard her, though they stopped with surprise at the stranger. The smell was everywhere.

"They have never seen other people," said Tinka.

Inside the building everything was a jumble on the floor, which was just dirt, and full of chicken poop everywhere. Tools and peat and a pile of branches and cow tethers and all kinds of things. A chopping block with a rusty axe in it, ruined firewood baskets, almost nothing usable and everything old and poorly made.

"Do you have cows?" asked Larus surprised, picking up a tether.

Tinka shook her head.

"We had one, but it died."

Larus looked around quietly. The mess instilled in him a sense of hopelessness.

"There used to be a goat, too," murmured Tinka. "But my mother said I should let it out and let it walk around free—just like the chickens."

"Why?" Larus was not used to hearing about a goat roaming around loose.

"Because—"

Tinka went silent and her expression closed down. Larus didn't pressure her, since now he was here.

"It disappeared," said Tinka. "I called for it for days and days, but it didn't come back."

"It walked around here for a little while," she said, "but then it was gone. Just like the chickens—there are only two left. Before my dad was buried we had the cow too." She sounded like it was something inevitable, and she spoke very softly.

"My dad buried it," she said.

"The cow?"

She nodded.

Sacks and old rags were piled up by the one wall. It looked like someone had been lying on them.

"Do you sleep here?" asked Larus surprised.

"I used to sleep with my mom, but now I like sleeping here best. With the chickens."

"Do you have any bedclothes?"

"Yes. They're in the bed."

"Why didn't you bring them out here?"

"Because—" Tinka went quiet.

Larus cringed. The room he had in the barn at Mistress's was nothing special, but it was elegant compared to Tinka's shed with rags and chicken poop in a big jumble. Even Hartad's pile of straw was better than this.

They walked back outside and Tinka led him away from the buildings, farther in among the trees, where there was an oval ring of stones. She stopped there.

"This is where my dad is buried," she said.

Larus felt the hair raise on his head and his skin tingle down his back. He had no doubt that Tinka was telling the truth.

"Why?" he said, moving back a little.

"This was the best place we could find," she said solemnly.

"People don't just get buried there where they live," said Larus, feeling more and more ill at ease.

"But we had to. What else could we have done?"

"The churchyard, of course. That's where—"

"My mom did it," said Tinka.

"By herself?"

She said her mother didn't think that she should watch, but she did anyway. "She couldn't lift him. She had to drag him along the ground, out of bed onto the floor and out here."

"Why didn't he get buried properly?"

Tinka gave him a sharp look.

"It was properly. She read for him and sang for him and then afterwards we put the stones all around."

"But why didn't he get buried in the churchyard?" Larus was still confused.

"Because we didn't have any money, and my mom was sick. And where were we going to get a coffin? And how would we get it there? And if anyone knew my dad was dead they would come and take us away and put us in prison or the poorhouse. My mom wouldn't have that. She wanted to stay here."

Larus had never heard Tinka say so much all at once, and he stared at her with a knot in his stomach. She had been walking around with all this inside her the whole time.

"Prison?" he asked.

"That's what my mom said."

Next to the ring of stones lay the beginnings of another hole, with a small pile of dirt next to it, but grass and weeds had begun growing both on the pile and down inside the hole. The shovel was lying there on the ground. Larus could barely look at it.

"Where is she now?" he asked.

"Inside."

That sounded very normal, and Larus exhaled.

"We can go in," she said.

He followed her back to the buildings, where the front yard was completely covered with weeds. Even in front of the door to the house there was high grass.

She walked through the little kitchen, where there was

ash from the stove all over the floor, and where meager kitchen implements lay in random places.

Larus held his nose. The smell was in here. This is where it came from. They walked into the living room, which was also messy, but in a different way than in the shed, and the floor was full of dirt that had been carried in over a long period of time. It took a while before Larus realized that someone was lying in the bed, or actually on the bed, with just a sheet on top. The head was covered up, but two yellowish feet stuck out the bottom.

He stood there for a few seconds motionless, while the truth seeped into his mind and everything began to make sense. Then he darted out the door and halfway back to the cows, where he stopped and vomited.

He kneeled on the ground as his stomach turned and turned. When he finally calmed down and could open his eyes again, Tinka was there standing next to him. Larus didn't know how long she had been standing there without saying anything.

"There is a spring just over here," she said, when she saw that his eyes were open.

Without answering, Larus stood up and followed her. He rinsed out his mouth and drank and washed his face and hands. Then he started walking.

"Where are you going?" Tinka sounded worried.

"I don't know. Just away from here."

She followed silently after him while he ushered the cows in front, and after they had walked a good distance to a place where the grass was lush, he threw himself down under a tree as a sign that here was a place they could stay for a while.

Almost inaudibly he said, "How long—how long has it been like that?"

Tinka understood what he meant even though he didn't say it directly.

"Since last winter," she said, "since before Christmas. My mom said I should bury her when the ground thawed out, but—but—" She started sobbing.

Larus turned towards her puzzled. He hadn't expected her to cry. She was so—so—. He didn't know how to express it. She never smiled or laughed. Then he thought: stone-faced.

"I couldn't," she said. "I was so tired and cold and the shovel was so heavy—but I had promised."

Larus took out his bundle and gave her the bread, all of it. He couldn't eat anyway, and since it had been inside the house, he knew it would be smelly. He was about to throw up again.

"You can have the whole thing," he said.

"But what are you going to eat?"

"I don't want any. I'll find some berries somewhere."

Tinka munched on the bread and stared into space.

After sitting quietly for a long while, she said slowly, "It was your idea."

"I know."

"Are you mad at me?"

"No." After a long pause he said, "It was just a lot worse than I had thought."

"I didn't know how to tell you. I couldn't bring myself to do it."

"You can't live there anymore," said Larus in a decisive tone.

"Why not?"

"You just can't."

"If you keep giving me bread and milk—I don't have anywhere else to go."

"You can't live there all alone."

"I'm not a-," her voice trailed off.

"You have to come home with me today."

"No, no!" she flared up in horror. "They'll take me away!"

"If you keep living there, you're going to die."

"I know."

"Aren't you afraid?"

"Not really—I don't know."

They were quiet for a while.

Then Larus said firmly, "Your mother has to be buried." Tinka sat there pulling up grass for a long time. Larus could tell it was sinking in.

"What if you helped me?" she asked, quietly and plaintively.

"No!" The word exploded from Larus like a horrified shout. "Never. I'm never going back there again." A bit later, after he realized he would have to force her into it, he said, "But I can go to the village and tell the parish chairman that she's lying there."

"Then what will happen?"

"Then they will come with a coffin and drive her to the churchyard and then you will get taken to the poorhouse."

"You don't have to tell them I'm here," said Tinka in her defense.

"They will see in the church record that you are."

"Not me."

"Why not? You get written down in it by the priest when you're born."

"Not me."

"Everyone gets written down."

"My mom said they didn't tell them about me."

"But they have to. Why didn't they?"

"Because then they would have to say where they lived."

"Couldn't they do that?"

"I don't know. But in any case no one knew about us."

Larus thought that sounded very strange.

"Why did they have to live in a place like that?"

Tinka shrugged. "I don't know. They just did."

"But in a place where no one else lives?" Larus felt in his bones how desolate that must be. Tinka didn't answer.

"You can stay in my room," suggested Larus. "Mistress has no one to help her. Maybe they will let you stay there."

Tinka didn't say anything, but he knew she heard him. And Larus kept talking, to convince her to go back with him.

"I'm not going to the poorhouse," she said.

"You don't have to," he said encouragingly. And gradually her resistance softened.

A bit later he asked. "What did you eat over the winter?"

"The grain. Just like the chickens. That's all there was."

"But now there isn't anything."

"Yes there is—all the berries."

"This winter there won't be anything. You'll die of hunger."

"Not if you bring me something."

"No one puts their cows out to graze in the winter," he said.

She hadn't thought of that. Tinka went silent, and the next time he asked her to go home with him she said yes.

He got ready to head back, because it was farther now than usual, and besides, he didn't want to risk her changing her mind.

It also became apparent that they had to take breaks along the way for Tinka to rest. She wasn't used to walking so far, and she tired easily. But when they reached the village, she was so afraid she grabbed onto Larus. It took a while for Larus to realize that she was afraid of the village itself, all the houses, the size of it, its aloofness, and the main street.

"Walk faster," he said, "so the cows don't get away from us. It's not much farther."

Tinka had no choice. She was practically walking on Larus's heels out of fear of being left behind. Eventually they and the cows made it across the courtyard and through the open barn door. The barn scared her too. Tinka had never seen a room that large, so Larus pulled her into his room and told her to stay there and to be very quiet. Whatever she heard outside, she must not open the door until he came back. Larus thought that Master would probably chase her away if he found a strange girl looking like that near his cows.

Then he hurried over to Mistress, who could tell right away that something strange was going on. She was making bread dough, and Larus walked up to her, but he had trouble getting the words out. Everything seemed so overwhelming.

Mistress gave him a couple of looks, and wondered if

one of the animals had gotten hurt or run away. This was not a very good time to leave and go searching.

"What's wrong?" she said finally, to get him started.

Larus looked down and traced with his toes on the kitchen floor.

"Did one get away from you?" she asked.

He shook his head.

"Then what?" She stopped kneading the dough and looked right at him. He didn't look like he had been in a struggle.

"There's a girl out in the barn," he blurted out.

"What?" Mistress didn't know if she should believe him or not.

"I brought a girl back with me. She's out in the barn right now." Larus's feet fidgeted with fear over what might happen.

"What kind of a girl?" Mistress's voice was dismissive.

"A girl I found—her mother is dead and rotting in a house far out in the grasslands."

"But there aren't any houses out there," said Mistress.

"She's lying there rotting," maintained Larus. "She's been there since Christmas."

"But no one lives out there. There are no houses in the grasslands. You're making things up."

"I was there today." Larus's face went pale and he put his hand to his mouth and gagged.

"Hey there, boy." Mistress pulled her hands from the dough and pushed the wash bucket over to him, but he stopped gagging.

"Sit down here on the firewood box," she said. "Tell me from the beginning."

Larus did as she said, starting with the day Tinka showed up outside his cave in the pouring rain. He told her how she looked and how she smelled so bad he couldn't be near her. He was honest about giving her his bread and milking a bit from a cow for her to drink. He didn't hide a thing, but told her what happened day by day, ending with the house hidden in the trees and what he saw there. How she had been living in a shed on some sacks with two chickens for a long time, eating the same things they did.

Mistress removed the dough from her hands and washed them as he spoke, and then let them hang motionless by her sides until he was finished. Her face had an icy expression as Larus looked anxiously up at her.

"Let's go out and look," said Mistress. She was prepared for anything.

Out in the barn she looked quickly around, but there was nothing unusual. Without a word she followed behind Larus as he quietly opened the door to his room and looked in.

It was empty.

The void made Larus go weak, and he turned right around towards Mistress to assure her—to swear if he had to—that he wasn't lying.

But Mistress put her finger admonishingly on her lips and shushed him. She could see what he couldn't from his much lower vantage; she was looking into the deep and poorly filled bed frame.

"Oh my God," she said.

Larus looked over and saw Tinka down under the comforter, sleeping with her filthy hands on either side of her dirty face.

"What a stench," said Mistress, holding her nose. "That's what I was smelling on you before. Now it starts to make sense."

Down on the bedstraw Tinka began to stir and opened her eyes with the woman bent over the bed.

"Mommy!" she exclaimed and sat up.

Then she realized her mistake and started crying pitifully while Mistress backed away from the smell with grimaces of disgust. The child was so indescribably filthy that Mistress stood there looking down at the sobbing Tinka without be able to bring herself to do anything else.

"First we have to get that child washed. We can't bring her anywhere the way she looks and smells."

"Get up," said Mistress.

This was addressed to Tinka, who automatically obeyed.

Larus thought that she had probably never seen another grown woman other than her mother, which seemed strange.

"You had better come too," said Mistress over her shoulder to Larus, as if she was afraid to be alone with the strange child. Meanwhile she prodded Tinka out of the barn and into the yard.

"Don't be afraid," she murmured.

"We aren't going to hurt you."

Inside the scullery, Mistress told Larus to pull the washtub out onto the floor, while she went over to the stove to pour steaming hot water from the water pot into a pail. She carried it to the basin and poured it in. The steam roiled up like a thick cloud under the ceiling in the chilly room.

"Now take off your clothes, little one," she said to Tinka as she went past.

"Are you going to boil me?" whispered the frightened child.

"How could you think such a thing," said Mistress flatly. "Here we are trying to help you from the goodness in our hearts to get the filth off of you, and you say something like that." She walked past the child with a bucket in each hand, and filled them outside.

"Have you never had a bath?" she asked when she came back inside, emptying one of the buckets in the tub.

"I don't know," whispered Tinka. "Not like this."

"Just take off your clothes," repeated Mistress.

Tinka fumbled with the buttons.

"Larus, you have to help her. You can have a hot bath afterwards if you do this for me. I can't bring myself to touch her."

The woman washed her hands in the tub and filled the pot on the stove again before she turned back to the dough, and Larus painstakingly removed Tinka's clothes and let the pieces fall to the floor around her. She was wearing more than he thought, layer upon layer, all of it brownish black with old filth.

As she punched down the dough and formed the loaves, the woman turned slightly towards Tinka and said, "Now into the tub with you."

Tinka hesitantly stuck her one leg dubiously over the edge before following with the other. Then she sat down in the water with a relieved look on her face.

"Get down well into the water to loosen the dirt up," said Mistress while finishing the loaves.

"And you come here with her clothes," she said to Larus while lifting up the stove covers.

Larus gathered the clothes together and dumped them down into the flames without paying any attention to Tinka's horrified expression.

"My clothes!" she protested. "What am I going to wear?" "We'll figure that out," said Mistress from the kitchen, "and if you are a good girl and don't cry you'll get a big piece of bread with butter on it when they're done."

Tinka looked from Mistress to the rising loaves and went silent. The woman slid them into the oven and closed the door.

Then she walked out to the scullery with a scissors in her hand.

"I'm going to cut off the worst of it," she said, bending over Tinka's hair. "I've never seen a rat's nest like this."

Tinka thought about the bread and let her hair get cut without complaining. But there was evidently a lot that was the worst of it. Clump after clump fell to the floor until she thought there was barely any hair left on her head.

"Toss that in the stove too," said Mistress to Larus, pointing with her foot at the hair she cut off. "I'm going over to Erna's to hear if I can borrow some clothes from her—and you scrub her while I'm gone."

On the way out she took the pail of soap and a brush and handed it to him. "I'll be back soon to change the water," she added, before disappearing out the door.

"Stand up," said Larus.

"Why?"

"I have to scrub you."

"I would rather wait until she comes back."

"You won't get any bread if you make a fuss," said Larus. Tinka stood up obediently. Larus took some of the brown soap from the pail and rubbed it on her. She was even skinnier to the touch than she was to look at, he thought to himself. He could feel her bones right under his hands.

Then he started with the brush.

"Not so hard, not so hard," moaned Tinka, and Larus let up a bit. The water went totally brown, but her skin got lighter. Finally he soaped her hair, though there wasn't much left on her head, and it foamed up grayish brown beneath his fingers.

"You're turning blonde," he said surprised. "Your hair is blonde underneath."

"I just thought it was the way it was," said Tinka, feeling the top of her head.

She went down into the water and sat there, waiting, until Mistress came rushing in, and before even putting down the pile of clothes, hurried over to check on the bread. They must have been fine, because she turned back to Tinka and told her to step out onto the floor while she and Larus carried the tub outside and dumped it out.

As she walked over with new hot water from the stove, Mistress said approvingly, at the sight of Tinka, "Now you are a few shades lighter. This time I can wash you, and Larus will have to go out and deal with the cows himself today." Larus nodded and did as she said.

When he came back inside, Tinka was sitting on the firewood box, bright and fine and in new clean clothes, eating the bread which she got as a reward for not crying while she was being washed. Mistress had scrubbed her a second time and cleaned out her ears and behind her ears, and scoured her with the brush and rag until her skin was burning. The used water was still in the basin on the floor.

They emptied it out once again, and Larus got new water, as Mistress had promised, and he happily climbed into it.

IV

"We'll eat as soon as I get back," said Mistress, wrapping a shawl around her shoulders. "I have just enough time to walk her over there."

This made Larus jump, so water sloshed out onto the floor.

"Over where?" he asked anxiously.

"Over to the parish chairman of course. She has to be reported and written up and such."

Tinka tried to protest, but Mistress took her by the wrist and led her down from the firewood box where she was about to fall asleep, and out the door.

Confused and alarmed, Larus quickly finished washing himself. What was going to happen now? He thought as hard as he could, but got nowhere, and while he was still standing in the tub drying himself, Master entered the scullery. He bristled at the sight.

"What's going on here?" he growled.

"Mistress said I had to take a bath," said Larus.

"Why?"

"Because I smelled like death."

Master stared at him as if he wanted further explanation, and Larus continued.

"I found a girl out in the grasslands and brought her back because her mother was lying there dead."

"And that's why you needed a bath?"

"She was rotting," said Larus, and Master grimaced with disgust.

"And where is this girl now?" he asked.

"Mistress is walking her over to the parish chairman," said Larus. "We're going to eat when she comes back."

Master grunted and disappeared into the kitchen, shutting the door behind him. Larus didn't dare follow him in there when he was done with his bath. Instead he sat on the washing bench until Mistress came back.

She walked right past him.

Her face was stony and angry, and her mouth taut as a rope. It made Larus afraid. Where was Tinka? She didn't come back? He sat motionless, and she shut the door behind her as well when she went into the kitchen.

"Well?" asked Master.

"Unbelievable," said Mistress, with a voice that matched her angry face perfectly. "Here we do all we can to help the girl, and then we can barely get rid of her. We scoured her and scrubbed her, put her in clean clothes from Erna Aagesen—you have no idea how filthy she was when she got here. I've never seen anything like it. But do you think they will take her? He said straight out that I had to keep her until they looked into the parents."

"The parents? What about them?"

"No one knows who they are; they're not from here." Larus could hear Mistress plop down heavily onto a kitchen chair. "And the girl evidently doesn't know anything either, or she won't say. We couldn't get a word out of her. She just sat there staring, scared out of her wits—like she thought we were going to eat her—and then every so often she was about to fall asleep. From what Larus said, she has been living out there alone with her dead mother lying in bed for over six months."

"Out where?" asked Master.

"Apparently they tried to make a homestead all alone far out in the grasslands, and no one knew about it," said Mistress. "Idiocy. They buried the father right there when he died a couple of years ago. What the girl has been living off of goodness knows. It's a wonder she hasn't kicked the bucket, as little and skinny as she is with her bones sticking out everywhere."

"They must have been gypsies or the like," said Master dismissively. "What's he doing dragging one of them back here?"

"She doesn't look like one. She's very fair, even though she was pretty dark when he first brought her."

"But here—here with us?" complained the husband.

"Well, he didn't know what to do with her. I guess he could have just let her go and starve to death."

"It wasn't that bad, was it?"

"Well she was no bigger than a six-year-old. She probably hasn't had a decent meal since her mother died. What is there to live off of out there when the husband is dead? Amazing that she could stay alive this long."

Larus was standing up now, stiff as a statue, listening. His mind was dizzy with all he heard.

"But then they took her in?" asked Master.

"I had to force them into it. They said they didn't have anywhere to put her," said Mistress.

"Why couldn't they just put her at the poorhouse until they could find someone in the parish to take her?"

"Because she kept repeating that she wouldn't go to the poorhouse. It was like some notion she wouldn't let go of. Otherwise she had a very sweet face, once we got the filth off."

Master didn't say anything.

Larus was sweating under his clothes from nervousness. It was his fault, he was the one who pressured Tinka to come back with him. He had just about promised that she could stay here with him—and then Mistress had taken her away. Now she would probably end up at the poorhouse after all, or they would hold an auction for her, and whoever would take her for the smallest payment would get her as a maid to work and slave for her room and board.

He felt like everything was collapsing around him. He had thought Mistress would help Tinka and take her in. What should he do now?

Larus was feeling very uncomfortable during supper. He could tell that Mistress wasn't feeling too well either, as she avoided his eyes. Could it be that her conscience was bothering her?

Larus was sent out with the large clay dish to Hartad, which happened sometimes when Mistress had too much to do, though usually she did it herself, coaxing and babbling with her son in a way which Larus could never bring himself to do. He usually just put down the dish, like for a dog, and left again while Hartad ate it. Larus didn't think Hartad seemed to mind. The next day Mistress still had a taut expression, and Larus hurried off with the cows. When she was in that kind of mood it was best to get out of sight as quickly as possible. He went to his usual place and sat up in his cave while the animals grazed, but it felt empty without Tinka. It felt lonely, more than it did before he ever met her. He couldn't stop thinking about her. It was strange not having anyone to talk to.

Later in the day he heard voices and noise, and then a horse-drawn cart came bumping towards him with two farmhands on the driver's seat and two others in the back. They stopped in front of him by the cows and shouted up at him. They wanted him to come down. They had a coffin.

"Where is that house where people were living?" they asked him.

Larus pointed and told them.

"You had better come with us," they said.

"But I have to stay here with Master's cows," he said.

"Nonsense. You can come."

"No, I won't go!" he shouted.

Then they jumped out of the cart, grabbed hold of Larus and held him in the cart in front of the coffin.

"The parish chairman said we should ask you—we can't go searching around all day," said the man driving the horses.

Larus directed them, trying his best to remember the way. The wagon bumped and jostled along until he knew they were getting close.

"You can stop here and hold the horses," he said quickly. "It's right over there in those trees."

"We can drive all the way there," said the farmhands.

"Only if you keep hold of the horses," repeated Larus.

"What do you know about that?" the farmhands said, mocking him.

Larus went silent. He had warned them.

And when the horses a moment later reared up and pulled at the reins, so the men had to hold on with both hands, Larus used the opportunity to slide to the back and jump off. He hid in the bushes and saw how the farm-hands had to struggle with the horses, pulling them step by step between the trees which hid Tinka's house.

Then he hurried back to the cows and herded them farther away from the carriage track. He didn't want to talk to the farmhands or see their faces on their way back. But when he heard the rumbling of the wagon a while later, he also noticed clouds of smoke rising from the area where the house was located.

They burned it down. They had no right to do that. Larus stared in horror at the smoke. That was Tinka's house. Now her past was gone. No father, no mother and no birthplace.

A homeless orphan.

The words weighed on him, and he clearly imagined his own mother and father—and all his siblings—and their house. This made Tinka much poorer than him; she didn't even have her own clothes, only what was loaned to her.

From a distance he saw the horse and cart pass by with the coffin. The two farmhands who had been sitting on it on the way out were now walking behind it. Neither of them were saying a word, and they didn't look for him.

When he came back home that evening, Mistress was in her Sunday best and Larus realized that she had been to the funeral. The farmhands had driven the coffin right to the churchyard, where the grave digger had prepared the hole. Mistress told Master about it as if Larus weren't right there. "There weren't very many people in attendance," she said. "Just the farmhands, the parish chairman, and herself and Erna, who had loaned her the clothes."

"What about the girl?" asked Master.

"That kind of thing is not for children," she said. "It's best for her not to know about it until it's all over." Mistress's voice was dismissive, and Larus thought about what Tinka had said about standing and watching while her mother buried her father. He thought about how Tinka had tried to dig a hole for her mother, but was too small and weak to finish it.

"That is not for children." Mistress's voice echoed in Larus's ears.

Mistress said that the parish chairman had kept the child in his own home that night, but then she was brought to a place where she could stay.

The poorhouse, thought Larus, sighing quietly. He didn't dare say a word.

Two days later Tinka was lying in his bed when he went out to the barn to sleep, and he let out a yelp of surprise.

Tinka shushed him.

"What are you doing here?" he said with his mouth agape. "Where did you come from?"

"I ran away," she whispered. "I don't want to live there. Tomorrow I'll go with you back to my own house." Larus felt the air go out of him.

"But it's gone," he blurted out. "They burned it down. The parish chairman's farmhands were out there with a coffin to get your mother, and when they drove away they lit it on fire. I saw the clouds of smoke."

Tinka was very quiet.

"Where is my mother now?" she asked.

"I'm pretty sure they buried her," he said. "Mistress

was in her Sunday clothes when I got home. She told Master that it was not for children."

Tinka took a deep breath.

"I'm not going to live at the poorhouse," she said.

"I know," whispered Larus, feeling ashamed. "I couldn't do anything about it. I didn't think Mistress would send you away."

"Can't I stay here with you?" pleaded Tinka.

"But I have to go out with the cows," said Larus.

"That doesn't matter. I can be here by myself. I can just lie in the bed. It's so nice to have a bed."

"All day?"

"Just until we figure something else out," said Tinka.

Larus relented. He couldn't think of another solution.

"But what are you going to do all that time?" he asked.

"Sleep," said Tinka, stretching out happily in the bed.

"But remember about Hartad," warned Larus, recalling that he had told her about him.

"So what," she said.

"I have to go get more straw to put in the bottom of the bed," said Larus, "and I'll see if I can get something for you to eat."

"Are you upset that I came?" asked Tinka.

"I was upset that you got sent away, and it feels very lonely out in the grasslands without you there." Larus could tell that he was avoiding her question. Actually he didn't think it was such a good idea that she was there with him. He could get sent home if they found out.

The next day when he came back with the cows there was already a problem. Someone from the parish had come and told them that Tinka had disappeared, and they wanted to check if she had come back to the farm. Mistress was still pale and upset when Larus arrived.

"Do you think she went back to that house out there?" she asked worriedly.

"But it was burned down," said Larus. "They lit it on fire when they drove away with the coffin."

"Oh, no. Then she's just wandering around out there, the poor thing. I should have had the sense to keep her here until they found a place for her." Larus was surprised to hear Mistress blame herself for not being more accommodating. What could have changed her mind when she had been so determined to send the girl away? And she was in such a hurry to do it.

"Stop that nonsense," barked Master. "Your grumbling doesn't help the girl one bit. Her type is a dime a dozen—there are far too many like her. One more or less makes no difference."

"I can't imagine what it must be like for her out there in the dark all alone," continued Mistress.

"Then stop thinking about it. The wolves have probably eaten her already anyway."

"Wolves?" That gave Larus a start. "Are there wolves in the grasslands?"

Master tried to evade the question, but Larus couldn't help but think of the goat that disappeared and the chickens that became fewer and fewer. What if there really were wolves out there? He felt a cold tingle down his spine. He stared at Master, but the man just sat there at his place as if it were nothing to get upset about.

But Mistress couldn't help herself, and Larus realized that Tinka had been on her mind more than she had revealed. It was as if the spindly child in the washtub had touched something deep inside her, something she had tried to fight off and push aside. But with the thought of the little girl disappearing, it had risen to the surface. The girl whose hair she had cut because the knots couldn't be combed out, whose hair she had cut so close that the hair stood straight up from her head when it dried, like a bright golden fur over her sunken face. The child she had washed out of a pile of filth—the child she almost had created herself. Larus didn't say anything about this to Tinka. He didn't want to disappoint her again by dangling a brighter future in front of her.

The days passed.

Every evening Mistress asked worriedly if there had been any sign of Tinka at the places he had been with the cows, and he could truthfully say there had not.

No one in the village had seen the girl. There had been no sign of her anywhere.

Every evening Larus had his pockets filled with nuts which he had already cracked between two stones, so she wouldn't have to do it, and at every meal he put bread and potatoes under his shirt. And it was the plentiful time of year with apples, pears, and plums in all the gardens, so it was easy to get fruit for her.

And gradually Tinka got used to sneaking around inside the empty barn during quiet times when no one was around. But one evening Larus opened the door to let in the cows and he could tell right away that something was wrong. The door to his room was open, which was unusual, and Tinka was nowhere to be found.

Did they find her?

Had Mistress found her and sent her back to the parish? Or had Master? Larus's ears were hot with worry.

After he had put all the cows in their stalls and was starting to tether them, he noticed a rustling in the straw over at Hartad's bed. He looked over and saw that Hartad was there. He wasn't usually there this early.

Hartad was lying there holding something like one would hold a cat that was trying to get away, or a scared rabbit.

It was Tinka.

Her blue eyes were dark with fear, but she didn't yell or try to pull away. Maybe she did to start with, but against Hartad's immense strength, her weak struggles had no effect.

"Hey Hartad," shouted Larus, "what do have there?"

And Hartad laughed and lifted up Tinka, folded in his large hands, to show her to him.

"Can I try?" asked Larus.

But Hartad pulled Tinka close and babbled to her, just like his mother did to him.

Larus was shaking. Hartad could hurt her without realizing it, break something in her. Instead of trying to get her away from him, Larus let the cows be on their own while he dashed over to the kitchen, where Mistress stood preparing vegetables.

"You have to come right away," he panted. "Hurry."

"What are you doing here? Can't you at least open the door before you come barging in?"

"You have to hurry, please!" He was almost shouting.

"Calm down and tell me. What's wrong?" The woman stood imperturbably at her water basin.

"It's Tinka. She's over there. Hartad has her!" Larus shouted like he was talking to someone who was hard of hearing. Finally she started moving. The knife dropped from her hand and she started running with a carrot in the other hand. Larus jumped aside so she wouldn't knock him down. He didn't know the elderly woman could move that fast. She didn't really run, he noticed, but more skipped along and her slippers flopped, as she didn't stop to put on her clogs.

"Hartad," she roared, walking over to his pile of straw, "what do you have?"

He looked up guiltily and tried to hide Tinka. His mother was angry. That didn't happen very often, but right now she was terrifying. She stood over him with her hands by her sides and that voice—that frightening voice.

"Show me your hands," she said.

Hartad bowed his head and lifted his hands slightly, with his palms up.

"Higher."

Hartad lifted them some more. Tinka was lying curled up below him half-covered in straw.

"What did you find?" scolded his mother. "You know you may not take something that isn't ours."

Hartad whimpered and tried to defend himself with his strange sounds. Larus held his breath and didn't move.

"Come here, Tinka," said Mistress.

Tinka moved slowly and cautiously, her face was white and her eyes were wide. She crept nervously towards Mistress past Hartad's large body.

"Can you move a little faster?" said Mistress impatiently.

And Tinka tried to hurry, but just as she was about to

reach the manure trough, Hartad bent down and grabbed the girl by the leg, and he burst out laughing. Tinka squirmed and kicked as he howled with amusement, lifting her up from the straw.

"Give her to me," demanded Mistress.

But Hartad's large hand just swung the girl back and forth, and Mistress didn't dare to reach out for her, for fear that her son would throw her someplace. Then she realized she still had the carrot in her hand.

"Here you are Hartad, a carrot," she shouted over his noisy delight. "A carrot, Hartad!"

Hartad caught sight of the carrot dangling right near his hand. His face changed expression. This was food. He dropped Tinka and grabbed the carrot, and the girl fell headfirst down into the straw.

Mistress bent down slowly and pulled Tinka out to the feeding aisle, where she gathered her together like a pile of clothes.

"Take her out to the kitchen," whispered Mistress to Larus, pretending as if she were fixing up Hartad's pile of straw, while she babbled with him like she usually did when she was in the barn.

Larus picked up Tinka and carried her into the kitchen as Mistress had said. She hung like a rag doll in his arms, and he didn't dare put her down anywhere, but slid onto the firewood box with her. She didn't weigh very much. He was sure she was still as skinny and spare as the day he had scrubbed her in the tub, even though he thought she was eating more than before.

Was she dead? He was nervous.

A moment later Mistress came rushing in and grabbed

the large clay dish, in which she gathered leftover food for Hartad, and then she was gone again. Soon afterward, he saw through the window her shutting the hasp on the barn door from the outside.

Then she came back into the kitchen. Almost without breathing, and with shaky legs, she bent over Tinka.

"Is she breathing?" she whispered.

Larus didn't know and Mistress put an ear to the girl's chest.

"It's beating—thank God, she's alive." Tears flowed from her eyes as she lifted up Tinka and sat down in the armchair by the stove, where she rocked the child back and forth, waiting for her to regain consciousness.

"Little girl, little girl," she whispered.

Larus sat motionless on the firewood box, and couldn't believe his own ears.

"Here I was thinking you were lost in the grasslands, and that the wolves had eaten you," said Mistress. "And then you come back to me all on your own, and are nearly killed in my own barn."

Larus was silent. He wasn't sure if he should say that she had actually come back to him, and the she had been staying in his room and sleeping in his bed for quite a few days, and that he had been stealing food for her.

Tinka sighed, and it looked like her fainting was changing into regular sleep. She was breathing audibly now. Mistress stood up holding her.

"Go open the door," she said.

Larus did as she said and opened the door into the living room, a place he had never been before. There were several doors off of that room, and he stopped in confusion, but Mistress went to open the next door herself. She laid Tinka down on the bed and told Larus to stay sitting by her side until she returned.

Larus sat down, and Mistress hurried over to the barn to see if Hartad had calmed down. It wasn't long before Tinka opened her eyes, and Larus could see her gaze wandering around the strange room until she spotted him.

"Where am I?" she whispered.

"You are lying in Mistress's bed," said Larus.

"Am I sick?"

"Hartad caught you out in the barn."

Tinka gasped and put her hands up in front of her eyes.

"Where is he?" she murmured.

"In the barn," said Larus. "There's nothing to be afraid of now."

"I thought he was going to tear me into pieces and eat me," she sobbed. "Suddenly he came into the barn while I was there, and he grabbed me."

Larus let her cry.

"Don't tell Mistress that you've been staying out there this whole time," he said softly.

Tinka looked at him puzzled.

"She thinks you've been wandering out in the grasslands," he continued, "and that you came back to her."

"Is she mad at me?"

Larus shook his head. "She's been very sad," he said.

"Because I ran away?"

"Because she didn't keep you here, until they found someone who wanted you," he answered softly.

"I would rather stay here," whispered the girl from the bed.

Larus didn't answer. He didn't dare tell her that he thought Mistress wanted her to stay.

"What should I say when she asks me where I've been?" asked Tinka.

"That you don't know, or you can't remember, or something like that," he said.

They were quiet for a while. In the silence they could hear Mistress's clogs in the courtyard. Soon after, Mistress came into the bedroom and told Larus that now he could go back to the barn and work.

V

For a long time Larus hardly saw Tinka. She slept inside the house someplace, and she wasn't up when he left with the cows in the morning. She never came out to the barn, but he understood, since she had been so frightened that day Hartad had caught her, and Mistress had probably forbid her to set foot out there again. Mistress had been scared herself—Larus could see that her hands were shaking and her face was very pale, almost like wax. Hartad could easily have injured Tinka very badly.

The way it was now, Larus only saw Tinka at supper, and he couldn't really talk with her then, not really. And afterwards Tinka had to help with the washing, and all he could do was go out to his room in the barn. There was so much he wanted to ask her about; it had become so boring out in the grasslands now, without her. The other cowherds went other places with their cows, and besides, Larus had the sense that they were mad at him because he came from another village. The times he had encountered them on the village road they had yelled at him.

Sometimes he thought it would be nice if his father would come to visit him. He had promised to come if he could, but his father had only been there once, one evening, and only briefly. That was back at the start, before Tinka had shown up. Now Larus was hoping his father would visit again, but at the same time he knew it was a very long walk, especially considering both ways.

But then one evening, after she was done with the dishes, Tinka was sitting out on the kitchen stoop after they had eaten. Larus stared at her over from the barn. He figured it was a mistake on her part, and that Mistress would soon call her inside. But nothing happened, she just kept sitting there. Larus was tempted to go over to join her, but he didn't know if he should. Mistress had not spoken to him about Tinka since the girl had started living in the house. Maybe she didn't want him to talk to Tinka anymore.

He stood there considering, then he walked out to the well, to see if that would make something happen. He washed his face and arms while at the same time keeping an eye on Tinka on the stoop. She didn't move, but she watched him and smiled. Her hair had not grown out enough to settle on her head yet.

Larus wiped a couple of drops of water from his chin, shook the water off his hands, and walked resolutely over and sat down next to Tinka. But for a long time neither of them knew what to say, which had never been the case out in the grasslands. Larus sat there listening for any sounds from behind him inside the house, and he had the feeling that Tinka was doing the same thing.

"Are you allowed to sit here?" he whispered finally.

"I didn't ask," Tinka whispered back.

"What if she sees you?"

Tinka shrugged.

"And that I'm here too?"

"I'm not sure I'm going to stay here," whispered Tinka.

Larus turned and looked at her with a very concerned expression.

"But why not?"

"Because she's always taking care of me and watching

me. I can't do anything myself. She wants to decide everything about me, and if I want to go someplace to play, she follows me and brings me back. I can't go anywhere alone, not even if it's nearby. She wants to decide who I'm allowed to play with. But if she is going to always go around afraid that I'm going to run away—then I'm leaving."

"But you get food and clothes and everything," Larus protested. "What's going to happen to you if you run away?"

Tinka sighed.

Larus waited silently.

Finally Tinka said, "I asked if I could go to school."

"Aren't you allowed?"

"She hasn't said yes yet. It's as if she doesn't dare let me out of her sight for one minute. I always have to do exactly what she says, and only that. I would rather go with you out to the grasslands."

"Great," said Larus gladly.

"But I'm not allowed. I asked."

"Why not?"

Tinka gave a big shrug, and then let her shoulders fall again in despair. "I can't even walk to the churchyard," she said. "Mistress wants me to be her daughter, and forget everything else that ever happened. But a person can't just forget who they are. One day I'll come with you out to the grasslands again. It's been so long since I was there."

"What if she beats you?" whispered Larus with trepidation. "She will probably get very mad if you do something like that."

"She doesn't need to know where I am."

"You mean you will stay out there?"

"Of course."

"But there isn't any house anymore. They burned it down."

"Have you been over to it?" Tinka observed him carefully. But Larus shook his head dismissively. He didn't want to go there again.

When Larus didn't say anything, she continued, "So it's possible that the shed didn't get burned down."

"But you can't live there alone," said Larus. "How will you get food?"

"You can bring me something," she said calmly. "Just like before."

"What about the winter?"

"You can bring me something even though it's winter," she said.

Larus shook his head back and forth. There was a lot she didn't understand.

"I'm not here in the winter," he said. "I go back home—I go to school in the winter."

"What about the cows?" she asked.

"They don't go out when it's cold. Only in the summer when there's grass."

She looked at him with disappointment. Then she looked away.

"But maybe they will hire me back in the spring," said Larus hesitantly.

He didn't say any more, because over at the barn, the door slowly opened and Hartad bent down under the doorway and stepped outside. He looked directly at the two children on the stoop and began walking over. Tinka and Larus both stood up.

"Quick, go inside, he's coming over here," whispered Larus, who stayed standing there until he could hear that Tinka had disappeared inside the house. Then Larus reached inside the scullery and took an apple from the table in there. Then he turned to walk towards Hartad.

"Look, Hartad," he said, trying to mimic Mistress's voice that day she had saved Tinka with a carrot. "An apple, Hartad, an apple." Both authoritative and inviting, he thought.

The large, stooping man walked directly over to him, and Larus had to keep a firm grip on himself not to toss the apple and run away.

"Apple, Hartad. Apple," he repeated, holding it out in his hand as if to a horse.

Hartad reached his hand out for the apple as he kept walking, right past Larus, over to the stoop, where he sat down exactly as Larus and Tinka had been sitting just moments before.

He bit at the apple just like a horse, thought Larus. Half of it disappeared on the first bite, and he shoved the rest in all at once, stem and core and all. Then Hartad slid to the side and patted the stone step next to him. Larus realized fearfully that Hartad wanted him to sit down. Larus approached hesitantly, and Hartad's mouth smiled and laughed, which also sounded like a horse, thought Larus, who didn't know what he should do.

But before he had really decided, Hartad had lifted one of his long arms and grabbed hold of Larus's wrist, pulling him down onto the step next to him. Larus was scared to death at first, but Hartad let go of him immediately, shuddered slightly, and laughed and babbled. It was obviously a special experience for him to sit on a stoop next to someone else. He must have seen Tinka and Larus from the barn and he wanted to be a part of it.

Larus didn't dare move, but eventually, as the intent behind Hartad's behavior became evident, Larus settled down, and in the end he turned to Hartad and sent him an uncertain smile, which made Hartad screech with delight.

Then Mistress came rushing out of the house in her floppy slippers with a piece of fine white bread in her hand. She used the bread to lure her son back to the barn. As soon as Hartad saw the bait he immediately forgot whatever else he had been doing—sitting on a stoop with someone, like a real person.

Mistress stayed over in the barn until she was sure Hartad was sleeping. On her way back she told Larus, as she passed by him, that he could go to his room now. She didn't mention the stoop, but Larus was sure that Tinka would get a talking to about never doing that again.

When Larus was lying in his bed, he thought about how happy Hartad had been while they were sitting next to one another. Larus had never seen him so happy before, except perhaps with the exception of when he had caught Tinka and he was sitting in the straw holding her. Larus realized that he had never really thought of Hartad as a person who needed to be with someone else, but only as someone scary and dangerous.

Larus crept down under the covers and tried to sleep, but he kept seeing Hartad in his mind's eye, laughing, sitting on the stoop, almost triumphantly, because he was really there.

But if Hartad could be happy like that, then he must also be able to feel sad.

Larus thought about that a long time.

Did it make him sad when Mistress scolded him that day he was sitting in his stall holding onto Tinka? Maybe afterwards? Or did he just forget the whole thing when he got the carrot?

Or was he sad when he was out in the field gathering stones to carry to the wall? Or when he was alone digging up peat in the bog? Larus couldn't tell by looking at him. But Hartad had laughed out loud when Larus sat down next to him on the step, even though Tinka had disappeared into the house.

The next evening Hartad was sitting alone in his stall when Larus came back with the cows, and the commotion and splattering sounds of hooves caused Hartad to look up, right when Larus was standing in front of his stall. Hartad's heavy face with the coarse features turned right at Larus, and, seized by a sudden impulse, Larus smiled and lifted his hand in a kind of greeting. After all, they had sat together on the stoop the day before.

Nothing happened. The heavy face did not change expression, but turned slowly, following the cows as usual. Not until much later. Then there was a sudden exhilarating shouting coming from the straw pile, and when Larus walked out from between the cows to look, Hartad was sitting with his hand raised and his palm turned out towards him. Larus waved back, and Hartad laughed loudly.

Larus continued to tie off the cows and spread feed in front of them, and every time he entered the field of vision of the man in the straw, Hartad lifted his hand with great glee. It was making Larus feel a bit uncomfortable, but he didn't dare not return the greeting. Then at the moment Mistress entered through the barn door with her milking kerchief around her hair and the clay dish in her hands, everything was forgotten. Mistress fussed with her son as usual, and Hartad grunted with satisfaction as he gobbled down his food and let her comb his unruly hair with the horse mane comb. Larus was careful to stay out of sight until he was sure Hartad was asleep.

But the following day Hartad still remembered the game. He had learned something, and Larus didn't know if that was a good thing or not. Hartad was sitting up waiting for him when he came in. But what would Mistress say when she found out? Would she think it was more troublesome to have a son she had to wave to all the time? That is was easier if he just sat in his stall and didn't demand attention? Larus didn't know what to think.

For a few days Larus tried to keep his distance from Hartad as much as possible, to be away from the barn when he didn't absolutely have to be there. Then he wandered around out by the gate without really knowing what to do.

But this caused the other boys in the village to take more notice of him. They stared at him and whispered together, which made Larus creep through the hedge to the back of the barn. He didn't think they seemed friendly.

Then one evening they caught him.

They had divided into two groups and hidden themselves, and suddenly they jumped out and ambushed him from both sides. Most of them were older, or bigger anyway, than he was, and they surrounded him without actually touching him. Larus was afraid. He didn't dare say a word or try to get away.

After they had stood in silence for a moment, one of the bigger boys said, "You think you're special because you're not from here?"

Larus just looked at him. He didn't think he went around making himself out to be more than he was—why did they think that?

"Aren't you afraid that it's contagious?"

"That what's contagious?" asked Larus timidly.

"Mister Water-on-the-brain in there." The other boy made a motion in the direction of the barn behind them.

"Water?"

"Didn't you ever hear it sloshing around?" laughed one of the others.

Larus looked around despondently at the ring around him. They were standing tight together. Then he tried to gather his courage.

"I thought he was born like that," he said.

"It still can be catching. Why do you think no one ever wants to take care of their cows? So they have to get hold of a twerp like you from someplace else.

"Well we're not having any of it, so you can just as well run along before you turn stupid."

"It's not contagious," said Larus, thinking that his mother and father wouldn't have let him be hired here if they thought that.

The boy leaned in and asked him threateningly, "What about the other one who left?"

"What happened to him?" asked Larus, shrinking back.

The boy tapped on his forehead with a bent and dirty finger. "He went nuts," he said.

"But my father said—" began Larus.

"Your father is a goose!" yelled the boy.

"He is not!" Larus yelled back.

"If I say he is then your father is a goose." The boy stuck his face right up to Larus's nose.

"You're the one who's a goose!" yelled Larus, slapping the boy right in his face.

This was the sign they had been waiting for, and they all jumped on him at once.

"So you like to hit, you bully?"

They grabbed him by the arms and legs and shirt and all over and then they threw him to the ground.

"You're not going to get away with that," hissed one of them. They all jumped on him and tried to hit him. One of them was straddling his chest and smacking him in the face, so his head rocked from side to side.

Larus clenched his teeth and squirmed to get loose, but someone was holding his arms out to the sides. They were all laughing.

"His pants—pull off his pants," he heard one of them say, and someone moved around to grab hold of the string around his waist.

"No!" he screamed. "Leave me alone!"

Larus was in agony and he screamed as loud and shrilly as he could. Then a hand came down and filled his mouth with torn grass from the roadside ditch. He sputtered and spit, and if he could have reached anyone with his teeth he wouldn't have hesitated to bite. Desperation gave him strength he didn't know he had, and he lifted the whole group of them off the ground for a brief moment, to try to throw them off. But their collective power was too great. There were too many of them, and he sank back down. Exhausted and full of rage and hate, Larus wished his father would come just then. On this day, at this moment—but he also knew that wouldn't happen.

He kept spitting out grass and screaming as loud as he could as they started tugging on his pants. If they ran away with them, Mistress would beat him, he was sure of that. It wasn't part of his contract that he would get new pants, and she couldn't have him walking around without any. Besides that would be the shame of slinking away, wearing no pants, with all of them laughing behind him.

But it seemed that they were having a hard time pulling them off, because at the same time they had to be careful to hold him down. The boys were swarming all over and around him.

Then something happened which made the boys stop still, and for a second Larus dared to believe that his father had come after all. He opened his eyes just long enough to see the top boy fly in an arc off to the side and land with a bump on the road. The weight on him lessened and he was more able to breathe. Then he saw the next boy's terrified face fly away and land in the ditch. The others scrambled and ran to safety. Only Hartad was left, towering over him like a tree and whimpering like a little baby.

It had all happened so fast that Larus started to cry, a thin sobbing squeezed out of him and blended with Hartad's whimper. Larus wasn't able to pull himself together to stand up. Hartad looked incredibly tall.

They were alone.

Then Hartad bent down and collected Larus as if he had been a dead puppy, slung him over his shoulder, and tramped away the short distance to the gate and into the courtyard. There he met Mistress, who came scurrying because Hartad was not at his place in the barn.

"But Hartad! What did you do now?"

Hartad let Larus slide down to the ground feet first, as if that would be enough explanation. But the sight of the boy's grimy face and the sorry state of his clothing did not lessen her dismay.

Larus pitifully pulled up his pants and started to tie the string again. Then he realized that Mistress was standing there admonishing Hartad, whose heavy face became more and more dejected.

"But he didn't do anything!" shouted Larus. "He came and helped me!"

"But what?" said Mistress in disbelief.

"The other boys beat me up."

"What others?"

"The ones who take care of the other cows."

"Why did they beat you up?" Mistress still looked at him suspiciously.

"I—I'm not really sure. They said—"

Larus stopped and blushed.

Mistress kept her eyes riveted on him.

"Yes?"

Larus scraped at the ground with his toes in between the bumpy stones in the courtyard. He didn't know how to answer.

"What did they say? Out with it." When Mistress spoke in that tone, Larus knew there was nothing he could do about it. He couldn't talk his way out of it.

"That Hartad was contagious," he whispered. "That he was the reason no one from the village would work for you, and that I should run away home right now—before it was too late."

Mistress just stood there. It didn't seem like it was the first time she had heard something like that.

"And what did you do?" she asked soberly.

"I hit him. I hit him right in the face, and then they knocked me down and hit me and spit on me. They sat on top of me, a big bunch of them." Larus had to catch himself to keep from crying again.

"How many of them were there in this heroic act?" asked Mistress.

"Five, I think," muttered Larus.

Mistress pursed her lips.

"Go to the trough and get washed," she said, then she walked over to the barn with Hartad.

Larus did as she said. He had dirt all over and he felt spit on his face and in his hair. He dunked his whole head down in the cold water and scrubbed himself with his hands. Then he brushed off his clothes with his hands as best as he could, but it didn't help all that much. At any rate, Mistress didn't look too impressed when he went into the barn.

"What were you doing out on the road?" she asked him.

"Nothing," said Larus dismissively.

"Stay away from those boys," she said, clenching her jaw. "They don't know what they're talking about."

Larus thought it sounded as if there had been problems with those boys before.

In his cave of straw, Hartad sat keeping an eye on his mother, and as soon as she left, Hartad lifted his hand to wave to Larus.

Larus lifted his hand too, and they both laughed quietly. Mistress was probably going inside to tell Master what had happened, thought Larus.

Then he walked over to the windowsill and took the mane comb and pulled it through his wet, dripping hair. He noticed his hair had gotten quite long this summer. When he got home, when his father came to get him in the fall, his mother would probably say that he was starting to look like a girl and she would cut it short again. She usually cut his hair before he went back to school.

Hartad sat watching what Larus was doing, and at one point he lifted his fingers to his own hair, as if the sight of what Larus was doing made him want to have his hair combed as well. In any case, Hartad was feeling around in his hair as if he were searching for something.

Larus walked over and showed Hartad the comb. Then he started to comb Hartad's hair, and Hartad closed his eyes with delight, just like when Mistress combed his hair. Afterwards he wanted to hold the comb, but Larus was sure it would get lost in the straw if he let him have it. Instead, Larus combed his own hair upwards from his scalp into a point, and it stayed there because it was wet. Hartad laughed loudly at him, and Larus quickly combed it back down.

VI

Two days later, Tinka went out to where Larus was tending the cows. He noticed her light summer dress far in the distance like a blow to his chest. What happened? Why was she coming? His thoughts raced, but he didn't really believe that she had run away, even though she had said she would. He started walking in her direction to meet her. "Is something wrong? Are you coming to get me?" he asked, as she stopped, panting, in front of him.

Tinka laughed at his worried face and shook her head. Her short hair was illuminated in the sunshine.

"Then what? Did you get permission to come out here?"

She shook her head again. "I just wanted to," she said lightly.

Larus stared at her. "That wasn't a very good idea," he said.

"Why not? I can't just go around doing exactly what she says all the time."

"Mistress?"

"She wants me to call her Mother—Mother Nana." Tinka spoke with a slight sneer and her words hung in the air for a while between them, while Larus weighed what she really meant by it.

"And you don't want to do that?" he asked carefully, when he couldn't reach any conclusion himself.

"She isn't my mother," answered Tinka angrily.

"But she wants you to be like her daughter?" said Larus, noticing a sinking feeling in his belly when he said it.

"I'm never allowed to do anything myself," grumbled Tinka.

"But you'll be the daughter of a farmer," replied Larus in disbelief. "You can have everything—nice clothes, good food, everything."

"Would you trade your mother for that?"

Her question made Larus go quiet for a while.

Then he replied, "It's not the same thing. Your mother died. Mine is still alive."

"She is still my mother. I went and visited her at the churchyard, even though I'm not allowed."

"How did you know where the grave was?"

"I just asked the grave digger."

"I hope you don't get beaten when you get home."

"If I do I'll run away. Far away. She has no right to hit me."

"Far away like your father and mother did? They didn't want anyone to decide over them either, which is probably why they moved all the way out here where no one else lived."

"How do you know?" Tinka narrowed her eyes and peered at Larus suspiciously. "Who told you that?"

"Or did they do something wrong they could get punished for? Like stealing or murder or something?"

"You are so mean."

"But robbers and murderers always live in deserted places," he continued.

"Who told you that?" she yelled angrily right in his face. "Who told you they killed somebody?"

Larus was taken aback by her ferocity.

"No one," he blurted out.

"Then why are you saying that?"

"I'm just guessing." Larus didn't dare tell her that he

had heard Mistress and a neighbor's wife talking about it, back when Tinka had been sent to the parish.

"Did your mother never tell you anything like that?" he asked.

Tinka shook her head and starting walking slowly towards the cows.

"Have you been back to see the house?" she asked out of the blue.

"Nah," said Larus.

"Why not?"

"Why would I go there? It's burned down."

"How can you know if you haven't actually been there?"

"I saw the smoke the day they did it," he said.

"Let's go over and see," suggested Tinka, as if it were the most natural thing in the world. She didn't waver one bit, and Larus shrank back. He didn't want to.

"Right now?" he asked.

Tinka felt his hesitation. "I could also just go by myself," she said. "You don't have to come."

Larus turned towards the cows. He didn't want her to go alone.

"I can come," he mumbled, with his back still to her.

Together they gathered in the cows and herded them, and as Larus walked he thought that he would stay with the cows when they stopped because of the smell. His stomach was already turning at the thought of that smell. But he kept walking, trying to decide what he would do, when he realized that they had walked nearly to the place where the house had stood, and the cows hadn't even noticed. He turned surprised towards Tinka, but she was too busy peeking in around the trees. All her attention was drawn towards the place where her home once had stood, and she walked closer to the site.

Larus stood back, watching her, then he left the cows chewing the untouched grass, and slowly walked over to her.

Tinka was standing at the edge of the clearing, staring at the house which was no longer there. Only a large burned spot on the ground, full of ash and charred ends of wood, was left. Larus stood next to her.

"But the other building," she said to herself. "The shed."

Now Larus realized that the burned spot wasn't everything, that the shed over between the bushes on the other side was still there. Tinka walked in an arc around the burned ruin and walked right into the shed and disappeared. Larus listened for the cows before following after her. It didn't smell any more, he thought. It was burned and blown away. It just smelled like after a fire. Inside the shed it looked as he remembered it—one big mess.

"They're gone," said Tinka.

Larus knew right away she meant the chickens, the two chickens she had lived with, eaten with and survived with. This made him think of what Master had said about the wolves, and Larus shivered.

"Shouldn't we go now?" he asked hoarsely.

"But we just got here," said Tinka.

"But there's nothing here."

"We don't know that yet. We haven't even looked." Tinka's voice was slightly reproachful.

Larus stood nervously shifting his weight. He didn't like being there, but it didn't seem to bother Tinka at all. Though maybe she didn't know about the possibility of wolves. She kept walking around and looking.

"Hurry up," whispered Larus.

"What are you afraid of?"

"Once Master said there might be wolves out here."

Tinka quickly turned to face him. She laughed. "Do you really think he would send his cows out here if that were true? Day after day?"

"Well, then what got the chickens?" said Larus in his defense.

"Foxes of course—or birds."

"Birds?"

"Big ones can—but usually it's foxes that do that."

Tinka walked out the shed door and directly over to the ash pile. Larus followed reluctantly behind.

"You can just go out to the cows if you don't want to be here," she said without even looking at him. She had already bent her head towards the ground, walking slowly around. The entire house had been made of wood, and there wasn't much left sticking up. Only the hearth had been built of stone and clay, which lay like a bump in the burnt remains. A piece of the chimney stuck up a bit higher, but the upper parts were broken and strewn on the ground around the hearth. Tinka kicked at the ashes and found a few sooty household articles: a milk jug, some pottery shards and two knife blades with their handles consumed by the fire. Larus didn't understand what she wanted with all that, but she swept away ashes and charred wood from the hearth and put down on it what she had found. The clay pot for cooking had been broken when the roof caved in, but still Tinka gathered all the pieces and laid them next to the other things she had found.

"What are you going to do with all of that?" asked Larus, who had slowly approached the ruin, and now stood on the perimeter of the burned remains.

"Nothing, it's just mine," said Tinka, picking up the end of a fire poker.

"It can't be used for anything," said Larus.

"It's still mine," said Tinka.

Larus thought to himself what he might find if it had been his mother's and father's house which burned down. What if he found the pot his mother always made porridge in? His belly tightened at the thought—but still it was difficult to see what purpose there was in the remains Tinka was collecting.

"Can we go now?" asked Larus impatiently.

"Okay," said Tinka, "in a little bit. You go and I'll catch up to you."

Larus stood there.

Tinka began picking up the things she had found and carrying them over to the shed. It took her three trips. Then she closed the door and slipped a stick into the hasp. She seemed satisfied, thought Larus, maybe because the shed was still there. But what was she going to do with all the things she found? They had no value at all. And she had gotten all black, not just on her legs and hands, but her dress was no longer bright and clean, as it was when they arrived. He dreaded bringing her back to Mistress the way she looked, and when they came to the creek he told her to get washed.

She spent the rest of the day picking flowers. But it was late in the summer and there weren't very many at that time of year. Still she kept walking around searching, and in the end she did collect a reasonable bouquet.

"Are you going to bring them back with you?" asked Larus.

"Why else do you think I would pick them?" she said.

"For Mistress?" Larus said hopefully. Maybe that would soften their arrival.

"For the grave," said Tinka, as if he could have figured that out for himself. "All the other graves had flowers," she said.

Larus's hope collapsed, and he prepared himself for his own share of the talking-to. Mistress would probably think he had asked Tinka to join him. He was very quiet on the walk home.

And if he had hoped that he could sneak into the barn by hiding among the cows he was wrong. As soon as they entered the courtyard, Mistress was standing there waiting, and she grabbed Tinka by the arm—you stay right here—and then she reached for Larus and pulled him over next to the girl. The cows had to go in and find their stalls on their own.

"What in the world got into your head that you drag her along with you out in the grasslands," she began in a foreboding tone. "We have been looking for her all over the village the whole day."

Larus stared guiltily down at the ground. What should he say? What could he say? He couldn't collect his thoughts. But before he got his mouth opened, he heard Tinka's confident little voice.

"He didn't drag me out with him." she said plain and clear.

"He didn't? Then how did you get out there, may I ask?"

"I walked by myself."

"You're lying. You can't find your way out there all alone."

"Of course I can. There are cow tracks the whole way." Mistress went silent and took a good look at her.

"Look at your clothes. What have you been doing?"

"I was searching around in the ashes."

"Ashes?" Mistress sent Larus a questioning look, but he pretended he didn't notice. "What ashes?"

"Where they burned my house down." There was no refuting Tinka's voice. She knew it was her right.

The color of Mistress's face turned a shade redder.

"Are you standing there telling me that you have been rooting around there where—there where—oh, God, how disgusting." Her voice cracked with revulsion.

"There where I used to live—yes," said Tinka.

"But you didn't really do that, did you?" If Tinka had told her that she had been rooting around in the manure pit, Mistress could not have been more shaken.

"What is so wrong with that?" said Tinka.

Larus was dumbfounded. Wasn't Tinka afraid of what they would do to her? Of being punished? She sounded as if she didn't care at all. He would never have dared to speak to Mistress like that—not even to his own mother. His father would have beat him if he heard that.

"But don't you understand—that smell—that horrible smell—" It was evident Mistress was despairing over the prospect of having to clean and scrub the girl again. On a proper farm one could not have children who smelled putrid.

"There isn't any smell out there anymore," ventured Larus.

"Is that so? So you went along with her over there?"
Mistress lashed out like a broody hen. Larus looked down
at the ground again and wished he could become invisible.

"I asked him to come with me," answered Tinka on
his behalf.

"So you left your duty with the cows?"

"We took them with us," Larus blurted out.

"That doesn't make it any better," continued Mistress.
"Why can't you stay away from that place? And you should
have asked permission to go out there." She gave Tinka's
arm a shake.

"Would I have been given permission?" Tinka looked
intensely at Mistress, who was taken aback and couldn't
answer.

"Can I go back out there tomorrow?" asked Tinka,
when Mistress didn't say anything.

"No, you may not in any way, shape or form. Look how
dirty you got!"

"Now you see why," said Tinka bitterly. "When I ask
I'm not allowed. I have never been allowed to do anything
I asked."

"What nonsense. You can do whatever you want."

"Can I go out and play with the other children on the
street?" Tinka wasn't going to let her off that easy.

"I told you before. You have to tell me which children
you are going to play with," said Mistress firmly.

"Can I start going to school?" continued Tinka un-
daunted.

"You know very well that I am not in favor of that. You
do not have to go to school, not yet anyway."

Tinka took a deep breath.

"In that case I will decide for myself when I want to go with Larus to the grasslands," she announced.

"But my dear child, don't you appreciate one bit how we are taking care of you? That we provide you food and clothes and a decent place to sleep. What would happen to you if we didn't give you a place to live?"

"I would go to the poorhouse," said Tinka without hesitation. "And when I run away from there I would be eaten by wolves."

"For heaven's sake, child, don't ever say such a thing!" Mistress put her hands up to her face in an attempt to erase the image of Tinka in the mouth of a wolf.

The girl paused.

Then she said, "Is it alright if I go put these on the grave?" She held out the wilted bouquet.

Larus could see the distaste evident in Mistress's face. She didn't want to say yes to that either, but she kept herself in check and nodded.

"Will you be back for dinner?" she asked.

"Yes, Mother Nana, I'll be home for dinner," answered Tinka gladly.

Astonished, Mistress watched Tinka skip out through the gate to the village street. For days she had struggled to elicit a shred of friendliness from the girl for everything she thought she was doing for her—a smile, a bit of gladness—instead of the constant reserved politeness. And then here, when she least expected it, a happy smile and a cheerful promise.

Mistress was silent and pensive the whole time she and Larus helped each other with the cows and the four small calves who were in an enclosure for themselves and didn't go out to the grasslands. Larus didn't interrupt her thoughts; he had also been witness to Tinka's surprising turnaround.

At dinner the otherwise unforthcoming Tinka told about the grave digger who was raking the churchyard when she arrived. Master lifted his head and gave a reproachful look to his wife; hadn't they agreed to keep the girl away from that churchyard? But Mother Nana was too engrossed in the girl's story to pay attention to anything else.

"He promised to write my mother's name on a board and put it on the grave," said Tinka, shoveling in her food with an eager appetite.

"So you do know your mother's name?" exclaimed Mistress without thinking.

Larus was startled at the sharpness in her voice, and Tinka's happy face closed up and changed to a frightened expression, as if she had said something she shouldn't have. Larus felt so bad for Tinka he could barely look at her. Tinka just stared at Mistress.

"Why didn't you tell the parish chairman?" asked Mistress. "He wanted you to tell him that."

Larus pressed his toes hard against the floorboards in misery. She was wrecking everything, he thought. Why did she always have to be so mean, and now when Tinka was so happy. Then he thought about how he had been so uncooperative with Tinka out at the burned house, how plainly he had demonstrated what he thought of the place, how much he didn't want to be there. But it was Tinka's birthplace—or the remains of it. He felt ashamed and kept his eyes on his plate.

Tinka was silent so long that Larus finally had to lift his head. Her eyes searched in bewilderment among the people at the table: Master who never really reconciled himself with her existence, Mistress who felt hurt because Tinka had kept a secret from her, and Larus himself who was wriggling like a worm under the circumstances.

Without a word Tinka dropped her spoon on her plate and lowered her head so far that her face was hidden from view. But she was crying. Larus was sure she was crying, even though he couldn't hear it, because tears were falling into her lap. Then she slid from her chair and in one continuous motion she slipped out the door and was gone.

Larus and Mistress stood up at the same time.

"Sit down," ordered Master. "Don't go running off in a frenzy just because a little girl is in a mood. She'll come back on her own. Finish eating." They sank down again onto their chairs and bent over their food, but they didn't taste it anymore. Neither of them were sure Tinka would come back, and each of them wondered where she would go, and Larus was sure she was on her way back out to the burned house. She seemed so at ease when she was there, and there once was a time when she didn't mind living in the shed. And she had placed her collection of burned treasures in there so carefully. Larus was certain she was going back there, and as soon as Master had said thank you for the meal and left the kitchen, Larus told Mistress that he was going to try to bring Tinka back.

"But she must know it's going to be dark soon," said Mistress. "It's not the middle of summer anymore. It would be crazy to walk out there so late." Larus could hear that Mistress was worried and sad.

Larus glanced out the window. The sun was not down all the way.

"Maybe she went back to the churchyard." continued Mistress softly. "I'll go over there and look—I'll ask the grave digger too, since he talks to her apparently."

Larus hadn't thought of the churchyard. There was no shelter there, and if she really wanted to run away, that wouldn't be a very good place. But it was nice of Mistress to go look. You could never be sure with Tinka. He took another glance at the sun and rushed off.

He ran the entire first stretch, and since he thought he was a better runner than Tinka, he kept expecting to see her little form come into sight. But Tinka was nowhere to be seen, and when he made it out to the area where the cows grazed, the sun had disappeared.

Larus stopped, breathing heavily, and he looked in the fox hole, well knowing that as long as she had the shed, she wouldn't be satisfied in that little cave. Deep inside he knew that he was just stalling, because he was reluctant to go back to the burned house, and especially to go back to the shed.

But he had to do it, and he had to hurry. The dark was deepening under the bushes and between the trees, and soon it would be very dark. He tried to pull himself away. Finally he convinced himself that if he ran very fast, then nothing waiting in ambush in the bushes would be able to jump out and grab him. And he set off at full speed.

But when he neared the trees around the homestead he stopped. There behind the burned spot was the grave of Tinka's father—not on blessed ground and without the help of a priest. What if… Larus felt fear holding him back. He wanted to turn around, but he couldn't go back home without even trying to look.

He pulled himself together one more time and ran over to the shed and pulled on the door. It was locked.

"Tinka," he called hesitantly, looking around to all sides.

No one answered.

"Tinka." He called a bit louder, and shook the door. She couldn't have fallen asleep that fast.

Then he realized the door was locked from the outside with the stick Tinka had put there. She wasn't there. He was all alone, and it was a long way back to the village.

With his gaze riveted to the place where the grave was, he slowly backed out of the homestead as quietly as he could, while at the same time he calmed himself by repeating that he didn't mean any harm, and that the man in the ground had to understand that he was just trying to help his daughter. He was just trying to bring her back.

He whispered this to himself as he walked backwards, on and on, until he backed into an elderberry bush and nearly fainted with fear before he realized what it was. Then he turned around and ran, crashing through the bushes and storming home with fear snapping at his heels. He had never run like that before. Even when he made it back to the village he couldn't stop. His legs kept moving, and he continued in through the gate, to the scullery door which boomed open and whacked against the wash basin, and in through the kitchen where there was still light.

Mistress jumped up from her kitchen chair at all the noise and was able to grab hold of Larus just before he collapsed on the kitchen floor.

"Oh my word!" she exclaimed, startled, and she kicked the door shut behind him, perhaps to keep out whatever was after him out in the dark.

Larus couldn't catch his breath. And Mistress had to wait for a long time before she could ask him anything.

"What was chasing you?" she asked.

"I—I don't know," he stammered.

"Well, what were you afraid of? Was it something about Tinka?"

Larus shook his head. "She wasn't there," he whispered. "The door was locked from the outside."

"What door? The house was burned down. You said it yourself."

"The shed. There's another building." Larus knew Tinka would be mad when she found out that he told Mistress the shed was still there, but he couldn't change that now.

Mistress sighed. "She wasn't in the churchyard either, and the grave digger didn't know anything."

"Can you stand up on your own now?" she asked, placing him on the floor away from her. Larus swayed a bit, but then he held onto the table edge.

"What were you so afraid of?" she asked again.

"I don't know," he muttered. "It felt like there was something in the bushes."

Mistress nodded. She understood.

"Are you alright going to bed now?" She looked at him carefully as he recovered. She didn't wait for him to answer, and she went to get a lantern from the scullery and lit it. "You can take this with you," she said, placing it in his hand and following him outside.

"Now be careful with that light," she said.

"I will," promised Larus, stepping down from the stoop.

VII

It was much later than Larus usually went to bed, and it felt strange to him to walk across the courtyard holding a lantern. It was like walking inside a cave of light, and outside the dark was pitch black, blacker than he ever thought it had been before when he had to go out and pee in the manure trench at night. But maybe it was because summer was nearly over. Larus thought that maybe he would be going back home to his mother and father again soon, but he didn't have a sense of the calendar, so he didn't know how much longer it would be.

He shone the light around when he entered the barn. The cows made giant shadows on the wall behind them when he lowered the lantern, but when he lifted it the shadows became small. It was so much fun that Larus almost forgot he was tired. But he wasn't allowed to play with the lantern, he knew that. Still he couldn't resist shining the light on Hartad who was curled up on his side without any covers.

He figured Mistress must have forgotten about his blanket when she went to look for Tinka in the church-yard.

Larus held out the the lantern to get a better look at the large person in his cave of straw, but then he jumped.

Held close to Hartad's chest, and almost completely covered by his arms and hands lay Tinka. She was sleeping soundly with her back towards Hartad's breath, which made her hair move gently to and fro.

Larus stood motionless with the light on them, then

94

he moved it away so they wouldn't wake up. What should he do? Tinka had gone into the barn on her own, he was sure about that. But how did she end up lying there with Hartad? Did she crawl in there herself or did he capture her? They looked peaceful enough lying there, but she was usually afraid of Hartad. Was she so upset by what happened in the kitchen that maybe she wanted Hartad to tear her to pieces right on the spot?

Larus didn't know what to think.

If he ran over to the house to get Mistress, there would be a big scene, because she would take Tinka away from Hartad and back into the house with her.

And what would Hartad do then? He didn't want to think about it.

But if he left them alone, then what would happen? That wasn't so easy to figure out. At least for Larus it wasn't. But as he stood there, full of doubt and confusion, suddenly he saw Hartad's one eye open. Hartad was awake, but he wasn't moving.

Larus didn't move either as their eyes met. Then very slowly and carefully Hartad lifted his one hand and waved to Larus like Larus had taught him. There was no trace of anger, no meanness, though perhaps a touch of anxiousness. It was clear to Larus that the large man had no intention of harming Tinka, and he lifted his hand in return. Hartad smiled and gently laid his hand down over Tinka again. Larus placed the lantern down on the floor and pointed questioningly towards the coarse horse blanket that hung on the wood partition.

Hartad gave a subtle nod, and Larus quietly laid it over them. Then he walked to his room, got undressed, blew out the lantern and crept under the blanket.

It was always Master who woke them in the morning—both Larus and Hartad. He usually opened Larus's door and shouted that it was time to get up, but Larus was not very quick to wake up. When he finally had rubbed the sleep from his eyes and got himself sitting upright, he could hear Hartad peeing in the trough behind the cows, And by the time Larus had fumbled his way through getting dressed and made it out into the barn, Hartad was already gone. He never really thought about where Hartad got his breakfast, but the clay dish was always lying on the scullery table, licked clean, when Larus went in to get his food.

But this day was different. Hartad was still lying in his stall when Larus came out into the barn. The large man looked up pitifully from the edge of the blanket without making any sign of getting up, and Larus was struck by a distant memory of what it felt like to get up after wetting the bed. He stood there staring, dumb and sleep-drunk, unable to gather himself, until he finally caught glimpse of the top of Tinka's hair just beside Hartad's head. Then he understood that Hartad didn't know how he was supposed to get up with Tinka lying on his arm.

"I'll help you," said Larus, slipping back the blanket enough so he could lift the sleeping girl. Hartad pulled out his arm and stood up while Larus placed the blanket back over Tinka. Behind him he could hear splashing in the manure trough, and then Hartad disappeared quickly out the door. Larus didn't watch him go, but siimply began feeding the cows like he usually did. For a little while he thought about whether or not he should wake up Tinka and get her to go back to her own bed, but he gave up on that idea. It was better to stay out of it. Completely.

When he returned after breakfast with Mistress on his heels, he hurried to take down the milking stool from the rafter and situate himself as far underneath the last cow in the line as possible. Mistress was going to feed the calves in the enclosure, but before that she usually hung up Hartad's blanket on the wooden partition.

Larus pressed his forehead against the warm cowhide and held his breath. He felt his heart pounding through his entire body.

Then it came—the scream. Mistress screamed, which made all the cows jump, and Larus found himself standing out in the center walkway of the barn without knowing how he had gotten there. If Mistress had found a snake as thick as an arm in Hartad's bedstraw she couldn't have screamed any louder. Larus went cold. Was Tinka dead? Had he squeezed her to death? That would be so horrible. But he didn't think that was... when he touched her...

Mistress stood with her arms hanging at her sides.

"Dear Lord, child, how you frightened me," she whispered, going down on her knees in the pile of straw.

And Larus went over to stand right beside her, and he saw Tinka sitting up in the stall, sleepy and with big terrified eyes. Mistress reached out and embraced the girl, and cried with a strangely raw and frightening sound which chased Larus back behind the cow. But he couldn't close his ears, and he had to go back to the pile of straw to look one more time.

Mistress sat there rocking Tinka back and forth, and the girl looked like she still wasn't completely awake. Her gaze wandered around the room as if she still wasn't sure where she was.

"You must never do that to me again," sobbed Mistress. "You must not come out here to him by yourself."

"But Hartad is nice," protested Tinka with a thin little voice.

"You don't know what you're talking about," said Mistress.

"He kept me warm all night," said Tinka.

"What were you doing out here?" asked Mistress. "Larus was in his room."

Tinka didn't answer.

"He caught you again?" asked Mistress.

Tinka shook her head. "He was sleeping," she said quietly.

"He was sleeping?" Mistress sounded surprised.

"And then I crawled next to him because I was cold, and then he woke up and held me very gently. Hartad is nice."

"God help us," sighed Mistress.

"I saw that time the other boys were beating up Larus," said Tinka. "Hartad came and made them scatter."

"How did you see that?"

"I heard them from the yard, so I snuck out to the hedge." "You keep away from them," admonished Mistress.

"They should just try and get hold of me," said Tinka.

"You talk real big," mumbled Mistress, rocking the girl back and forth.

"Once I bit a fox," declared Tinka.

"Sure you did. You don't have to make things up."

"But it's true. It came into the shed where I was lying and grabbed a hen off its roost. And I jumped on it."

"It didn't bite you?"

"It couldn't with the chicken in its mouth. I bit it instead."

"Where?"

"On its ear I think. It was something thin. It got so scared it clenched its teeth and killed the hen."

"How do you know that?"

"It stopped shrieking."

"And then the fox ran away?"

"It did, but without the chicken. I kept that."

"Did you eat it yourself?"

Tinka shook her head vigorously.

"That was Lillian," she said. "I buried her."

Mistress sighed again, and Larus was sure that Tinka was telling the truth. He could see the whole scene in his mind. And when the woman started clambering back to her feet again, he scrambled back to his milking stool.

"You had better come into the house and have something to eat," she told Tinka, and the girl followed her obediently across the floor. Larus didn't see Tinka again until supper, where she sat politely at her spot next to Mistress, as if nothing had happened the day before.

Master gave no sign that anything had happened either. But Larus figured he had already seen her at noontime and had been given some kind of explanation. He was a man of few words—usually anyway. But if there were guests and festive food and beer on the table, then he became talkative. Otherwise he barely answered a question, and definitely not if was just something routine. He was the most taciturn person Larus had ever met, and Master did not even offer a grunt to topics not concerning the operation of the farm.

Larus wondered what Mistress might have told Master. Did she even tell him that Tinka had slept with Hartad? Master resigned himself to Mistress's taking care of the girl, with the same indifference as if Tinka were a dog or a cat. And Larus could easily imagine, that while Mistress considered Tinka a permanent member of the family, Master considered her presence something temporary, like hiring a maid—or a cowherd for that matter. A person with whom it was not necessary to become personally involved—neither in joy nor in sorrow.

If Tinka had really disappeared or if Hartad had smothered her by accident, Master would have done nothing but shrug his shoulders. What mattered to him were his yields, the amount of peat and its dryness and thereby its fuel value, the condition of the cows and the reputation he acquired by having a good, well-run farm—despite the presence of Hartad. Hartad was a blemish.

Larus paused and held onto his last thought, turned it over and around. He had never seen it in that way before, not that clearly. But it had to be true. Hartad was a burden for Master's reputation. The way the village looked at the mentally compromised man had become evident that day the cowherd boys of the village beat up Larus and tried to pull off his pants. No one wanted to work where someone like Hartad lived. This must also affect Master's relationship to the other farmers in the area.

Larus sat at the table thinking about Hartad, who had been uneasy and restless since he returned from the bog. As soon as Hartad had come in through the barn door he had looked expectantly in his straw cave, and then he had walked all around the barn as if he were looking for something without really knowing what it was. He was missing something.

Mistress had gotten him to sit down and empty his clay dish as usual, but as soon as she was out the door again, his restlessness had him back on his feet. Larus had to shovel out the manure trench by himself. He didn't think he should get Master to make Hartad do it. And then from his seat on the bench by the wall, Larus could see the big man standing by the barn window as if he were waiting for someone.

Larus knew who he was waiting for. There was something in Hartad's face that evening which hadn't been there before—an expectation, a persistent yearning. Larus tried to avoid Hartad and mind his own business. Larus couldn't help him anyway.

Before they were quite finished with supper, Hartad bent down under the low doorway and stepped out looking to all sides. Larus went stiff and kept his attention on his plate. Master didn't turn his head and didn't notice anything, while Tinka and Mistress were sitting with their backs to the window. Larus couldn't help but see.

The big man walked carefully over towards the scullery door and out of view. But he didn't enter the house. Larus guessed that he had sat down on the stoop in an attempt to be with someone. Larus kept his eyes in his head and just listened. His ears felt large and open, but nothing entered them for a good long while. Then he heard a subtle scraping sound from the scullery, so quiet that only he noticed it.

Then the door to the kitchen opened hesitantly, and in the opening their son appeared, but without daring to come any closer. He had a sad expression on his heavy face. It was obvious he was afraid that he was doing something wrong.

Mistress turned her head and stood up halfway from her chair but was unable to push it out from the table. That's as far as she got.

"Hartad," she shouted, and sat down again.

But Hartad's yearning gaze had settled on Tinka by then, and he didn't hear a thing.

"Hartad," she roared, "go back out."

But Hartad just stood there, and Mistress's cloth slippers worked helplessly under her chair to get traction, while Master's eyes shifted between his weak-minded son and the woman who had given birth to him. He was waiting for her to get him out.

But before she was able to get her chair backed out and to stand up, Tinka had already slid from her chair and was on her way across the floor to the door, where she put her hand in Hartad's and walked out with him.

It was dead quiet in the kitchen. Each of them held their breath as they followed the dissimilar pair walking across the courtyard and into the barn. Then Master sat back down and returned to eating.

"Sit down," he said with his mouth full of food. And Larus and Mistress plopped back down and kept eating without looking at one another. Master had sounded more pleased than the occasion demanded, and his face was tranquil, as if someone had placed a large glass of schnapps in front of him. Finally he could see a purpose for the young girl his wife had dragged into their house. A babysitter for Hartad, a plaything for him, an orphan who wasn't too expensive to keep. He chuckled with contentment.

After the meal Mistress carried the leftovers into the pantry and signaled for Larus to follow her.

"Go out and look," she said quietly, out of Master's earshot. Larus walked over to the barn without answering.

The scene was the same as the day before, except it wasn't dark, and Tinka was playing a game with Hartad's fingers.

"Thumb," she said, waiting for him to stick out the proper digit.

When Hartad noticed Larus, he lifted his whole hand and made a bunch of noises as he laughed and grinned.

"Listen to me," said Tinka sternly, pulling down his hand. "Thumb?"

Hartad stuck out a finger.

But just that he knew what the game was about, thought Larus. Larus wouldn't have thought Hartad could have done that if he had only taken note of the way Mistress babbled with her son.

Tinka asked for his thumb again, and again got a finger. Then she showed him the right one.

"Try again. Thumb," she said.

This time he put out the proper digit, and Tinka was overjoyed. Afterwards she sang to him and Hartad fell quickly asleep. Larus knew the song because his mother had sung it to him when he was little—and Tinka's mother must have sung the same one to her.

When she was sure Hartad was fast asleep, Tinka said, "I'd better go inside now. Will you give me a hand?" Larus walked over and lifted Hartad's heavy arm which was lying on Tinka, and she crept out of the stall and helped him lay the blanket over the sleeping man.

"Do you think he can learn that?" asked Larus.

Tinka shrugged. "I remember my mother playing that game with me," she said. "He likes it."

Then she walked back across the courtyard. Master was still sitting at his place. The table had been cleared and the dishes washed, but Mistress was not to be seen.

"Where is Nana?" asked the girl, keeping a keen eye on Master's face, to see if he recognized the name.

He just grumbled and said, "She left. Just go to bed."

"What did she have to do?"

"Go talk to someone," he muttered, as if it didn't really matter. But Tinka got the sense that something was going on.

"Who did she have to talk to?" she asked.

Master said the name of a man, and something clicked in Tinka's mind. She thought she had heard that name before, and she repeated it silently to herself.

"Isn't that the parish chairman?" she asked.

Master didn't know what he should say, and he tried to deflect her question by saying he was a farmer with a lot of cows in his barn.

Tinka listened patiently to him until he thought he had led her thoughts off in a different direction.

"Why does she need to talk to him again?" she asked with a wrinkled brow and a sharpness in her voice. She was not going to be led astray.

Her questioning irritated Master, who was just about to inform her that it was none of her business, but he stopped himself, because he thought that would just make her even more determined to find out what the connection was. Or he risked that she would go and hide someplace, and he wanted no part of being questioned about that when his wife came home. So he just muttered something indistinctly, and Tinka sighed and laid her arms on the table top as if that had been answer enough. Master yawned and wished his wife would come back soon, so he could be released from sitting here entertaining this ridiculous little girl.

"Can't you just go to your room and go to bed?" he said.

"Sure," mumbled Tinka, lying her head down on her arms.

Master waited a bit, then he squirmed. "So off with you then, before you fall asleep right there," he said annoyed. But Tinka didn't respond. She took a deep peaceful breath, not bothered, since she knew he would never dream of carrying her to bed. Though he couldn't let her sit there all alone either. So there they sat until Mistress came home a bit later.

"You poor dear," she said as soon as she caught sight of Tinka. "Why didn't you tell her to go to bed?"

"But I did," he protested. "But she just sat there and fell asleep. Did you get anything out of him?" Master spoke softly, almost in a whisper, and Mistress slid silently into her chair next to Tinka.

"Maybe," she said. "In any case there once was a girl who disappeared from a village quite a distance from here. He didn't know if her name was Martha, but he would send a farmhand out to get more information. They never found her again."

Master cleared his throat, but then sat silently.

"It would be a good thing to know where she came from," said Mistress.

"Yeah, a farmer's daughter," muttered Master to himself. "A rich family with trunks full of dough."

"It doesn't really matter, does it, as long as they are proper people, that she doesn't come from a bad family," said Mistress.

Master puffed pensively on his pipe.

Then he said, "What do you think they would give to get her back?"

"What do you mean back? What are you talking about? She's never even lived with them." Mistress sounded offended.

"Instead of the daughter, I mean. The one who disappeared," he said.

Tinka gave a little jump.

"No, thank you very much," declared Mistress. "What are you driving at? That's not why I want to find out who she is."

"But don't you see?" Master sounded very pleased with his great idea. "The child is a cute little girl, and if you polish her up a bit—they can't assume that we would go through all that trouble for nothing."

"What trouble?"

"Giving her a roof over her head and feeding her, clothing her and everything like that—she's been here quite a while already."

"But I want to keep her here," said Mistress.

"Can't you hear how pathetic that sounds? What are you going to do with her? She doesn't want you as her mother. They would probably pay a hefty sum to bring her home."

"You never think of anything but money," hissed Mistress. "Besides, we don't even know for sure that their daughter was named Martha."

"It doesn't matter anyway," said Master with a sneer. "As long as they think it's her."

"It would be so empty here if she went away," sighed Mistress. "I have gotten so used to her being here."

"What does that matter if she doesn't like you," said Master. "She doesn't like it here, and she's only here because she has no other place to go."

Tinka was about to speak up in protest. But she caught herself and stayed calm. She did not like the way Mistress treated her like a little baby who couldn't do anything herself.

"You could have just agreed to have some more when we had the chance," said Master bitterly, as he stood up. "Ones that were our own."

Tinka's ears perked up. This was something she had not heard before.

"Did you want to have another one—like that?" said Mistress angrily. "I thought we agreed on that." She stood up too.

"And we are not going to have an orphan land in our laps again," she said. "You understand that, don't you? It's about seizing the opportunity."

Master started walking away grumbling, and Mistress bent slowly over Tinka and picked her up. She walked with her through the house to the little room which had been hers the whole time she had lived there. And Tinka didn't dare give away that she was awake, and that she had heard everything. It was better to wait and see.

A grandmother and grandfather? This is what she thought about lying in bed. Her real family? It was hard to believe; she never thought she had any other real family. Her mother's mother and her mother's father. She was already yearning for them.

VIII

Larus got water from the well and carried it into the barn, where he poured it out into the cows' troughs. It was heavy work. The yoke was too big and didn't fit his narrow bony shoulders. Even though he had shortened the ropes, the buckets still dangled so far down they scraped against the stones. Using a yoke like that was not worth it when it didn't amount to more than two half-filled buckets at a time.

He didn't understand why it fell to him to do it, since it had always been Master who filled the cows' trough—and did it before they came back.

He asked tentatively if Master was sick.

Mistress didn't answer. She just sat there with her forehead against the side of the cow, and a distant look in that part of her face he could see.

She looked strangely old, thought Larus. He wondered if something had happened to Master. Or to Tinka. But if Tinka were sick, she would have been kept inside. He wouldn't have been able to talk to her for several days. But she had been there at mealtimes, even though she had seemed very quiet, as if her thoughts were far, far away. Larus figured she was thinking about the house before it was burned.

He hung the yoke back up on the wall and took a bucket in each hand. That was easier. He still only filled them halfway, since Mistress wasn't watching, and besides, she didn't seem to care how many trips he had to make. It was almost like she didn't know he was there.

Just as he was pouring water into the last trough, Master's clogs came tramping across the courtyard. He was coming from the gate, so he had been out somewhere. Larus didn't have to look to know it was him.

Master entered the barn and walked right over to where Mistress was sitting, while Larus moved to a shadowy corner where there were no windows. Hartad was muttering to himself in his stall, fed and satisfied, and Larus didn't dare interrupt to ask what he ought to do next.

Master looked unusually bright, similar to when he had been to the market and made a good deal. He walked in and stood close to Mistress, his thumbs in the armholes of his vest, as if he were waiting for her to ask him about something. But Mistress didn't say anything; she didn't even turn her head. Though her hands stopped milking.

"They are going to come out and take a look at her on Sunday," he said, in a tone that matched his satisfied look.

Larus couldn't avoid noticing how Mistress's back collapsed with the news. It was almost as if he had hit her. Who were "they"? And who were they coming to look at? Had he sold one of the cows?

"Couldn't we just keep her now that we have her?" Mistress said softly. "Now that she's made herself at home."

"That's just what you think. A child like that is never going to feel at home anywhere. It's only a matter of time before she runs away, and then we're going to have to deal with all that trouble again."

It struck Larus that they were talking about Tinka. Were they going to get rid of her? And who was going to come and look at her?

"They are proper folk," said Master. "They are well-situated to pay for her stay here—and pay well."

"You never think about anything but money," said Mistress angrily. "Think about the child. Think about me if you don't care about her. I want her to stay here."

"A woman's flight of fancy," barked Master. "It'll pass. They're rich, you understand? They have the finest farm in their village. The girl will get anything she wants."

"Then why did her mother run away from home?" asked Mistress.

"Oh, it's the same old story, a farmhand, of course. She fell for a worker on the farm, some poor louse who had nothing to give her. I would have stood firm against that too, and so would any sensible family with means, that's obvious enough."

Master sounded like he had gotten a good bargain, while Mistress stared down at the hay on the floor.

"You said yourself it was good for Hartad that she was here," she muttered.

"Sure, but that was before we knew where she came from," said Master. "The way it is now we should get out of her what we can. Get that into your head."

Master squirmed uneasily at the sight of his wife's sunken figure, and then he caught sight of Larus in the corner. A sudden anger flared up inside him.

"What are you staring at?" he shouted. "Get to work. Get out of here and carry some kindling into the kitchen; the firewood box is nearly empty."

Larus sped out the door as if the devil were on his heels. Over in the woodshed he put some kindling in the basket, but before it was properly filled he ran over to the kitchen and emptied it. He had to talk to Tinka. He had to tell her what he had heard right away.

She was standing at the stove stirring the evening porridge. She had to use both hands because it was stiff and nearly ready.

"Someone is going to come and look at you," whispered Larus excitedly, keeping an eye on the barn door through the window.

"I know," said Tinka without looking at him.

"How can you know that when Master only just told Mistress this minute—over in the barn?" "Four days ago she went and talked to the parish chairman. He was going to send a farmhand off to look into it—so of course they want to see me, that's obvious. I'm their grandchild." Tinka lifted the pot out of the cooktop and put the cover on the hole.

"But—" Larus stared at her in surprise.

"It's because I told the grave digger my mother's name," said Tinka.

"But what happens if they want to take you back with them to their house?" gasped Larus, beside himself.

Tinka shrugged her shoulders and put the lid on the pot.

"Nothing." She tried to act unconcerned.

"Are you just going to drive away with them?"

"Maybe. They are my grandmother and grandfather."

Larus was shocked. "He said that he would get money for you," he whispered.

"Who?"

"Master. He wants to sell you."

"That's because he doesn't like me. If I come back it won't be because of him."

"Would you come back? Then why are you leaving?" Larus felt more and more confused.

"If I don't like it there, then I'll come back to Mistress." Tinka nodded resolutely, but Larus observed her with misgivings.

"What if you can't find your way back?" he asked.

"If you can go one way, you must be able to come back too," said Tinka. It sounded like she wasn't giving it any more thought.

"It must be very far away. I would rather that you stayed here," sighed Larus.

"Why?"

"Well, because I'm the one who found you."

"You aren't going to stay here either. You have to go back to your family," said Tinka.

Larus looked away—and saw Master coming out the barn door. He quickly grabbed the firewood basket and hurried out across the courtyard to refill it in the wood-shed. And this time he filled it all the way.

When he returned to the kitchen with the full bas-ket, Master was already sitting at his place at the table, and Tinka was in the process of setting it with plates and spoons.

As quietly as he could, Larus eased the basket con-tents into the firewood box and dashed back out. He could probably manage to fill one more basket before be-ing called to the table, since Mistress had not come inside yet. Larus felt a bit guilty that she had to do all the work in the barn herself, but on the other hand, Master had told him to leave and to fill up the firewood box.

Larus finished just before she came in. He was stand-ing just inside the door waiting, and Tinka was standing over by the sink. Neither of them dared to sit down before Mistress said it was time.

They both looked at Mistress when she came in, but quickly looked away again and pretended not to notice, though it was obvious she had been crying. Larus and Tinka traded a quick glance when she invited them to the table. Everything seemed so desperate when an adult was crying; it was so hard to witness. Feeling down-hearted, they placed their hands in their laps and bent their heads while Master said grace.

Then they ate in silence.

Afterwards, Larus hurried out to his room. He was afraid Mistress might start crying again, and he was sure that she didn't want him to see that either. He stood at the little window looking out on the manure pit behind the barn. He didn't feel like going to bed yet; there were so many thoughts tumbling around in his head.

Sunday was only a few days away. What if they really did drive away with Tinka? He felt miserable at the thought, as his room got darker and darker. Summer was ending too fast.

Then there was a noise at his door, and Tinka slipped in. Larus looked at her with surprise. Shouldn't she be in bed now?

"They told me about it. They don't know I heard the whole thing that evening when they thought I was asleep."

"What are you going to do?" asked Larus sadly.

Tinka gave a little shrug. "Nothing," she said. "Mistress is going to get me new clothes, so no one will be able to tell who I really am."

"Who are you really?" Larus didn't understand what she meant.

"You know." Her eyes widened in the weak light from the window.

Larus looked at her without saying anything. What did she mean by "really."

"Deep inside," she said, to help him along.

"How you are deep inside?" he asked slowly. "I don't know that."

"Do you think I can be made into a rich farmer's daughter by getting scrubbed clean and putting on new clothes? I'm not going to become a farmer's daughter that way. I'm always going to be Tinka who slept in the shed in the grasslands with the chickens while her mother was dead in the house. I'm going to keep on being myself, and my mother is going to keep on being my mother too, even if I get another one. Now do you understand?"

Tinka took a deep breath after that big outpouring, and Larus nodded mechanically and said he understood, even though he wasn't really sure. Maybe after he had thought about it some more and tried to imagine himself, and his mother, in Tinka's situation.

He just stood there thinking how strange it was that Tinka was so headstrong. If she didn't get things just the way she wanted them, then she wanted no part of it. But other eight-year-olds didn't get to decide for themselves; they had to do what they were told.

"Did your mother never tell you what to do, and things like that?" he asked carefully.

Tinka thought about it for a while. Then she nodded. "Sure. But I decided in the end," she said.

"But how?"

"She didn't check."

"Why not, when she told you what to do?"

"Because she was always lying in bed."

"No, I mean before she died."

"She was always lying in bed then too."

"Always?"

"She was sick for a long time. In the end she didn't even answer if I asked her something."

"Because she was dead?"

"No, because she swallowed the water."

"What water?" Larus was feeling uncomfortable with all this talk about death.

"The water I gave her, of course. I used the cow horn that I used when I was a little baby—it had a little hole in the tip."

Larus knew about that. His mother had one of those.

"Didn't she eat?" he asked.

Tinka shook her head. "Not towards the end. I had to take it out of her mouth, because she couldn't chew."

Larus was quiet for a while.

Then he said, "It makes sense that you want to keep deciding everything for yourself. But the grown-ups don't know that you can do that. There was one time when I tried to tell you what to do," he added with a crooked smile.

Tinka tried to see his face, but it was too dark. "When was that?" she asked.

"Back when I told you to wash off in the ditch. You were so filthy dirty."

"I didn't know I was; not back then," she admitted.

"I think it was good that I found you," he said.

"You didn't find me," said Tinka, and Larus could tell she was smiling.

"Then who did?" he said.

"I found you," she laughed.

Larus thought about the time he was in his cave and then suddenly she was standing down below.

"Right," he said. He had to agree with her. "But I did bring you home with me," he added.

Mistress called for Tinka from the courtyard.

"She's sad," whispered Larus quickly. "She wants to keep you."

Tinka nodded. "I have to go," she said softly.

The following two evenings Larus waited in vain for Tinka to come out and talk with him. And Sunday morning the wash basin was set out on the scullery floor when he left. She was going to get washed, he thought. She had to be made as clean and nice as possible, and then when he came back with the cows in the afternoon she would be gone. They will have taken her. They were coming to eat lunch and then afterwards—

Larus wandered around restlessly among the animals the entire morning. He kept glancing up at the clouds for the place where the sun was hiding, to see when it would be noon. They were going to drive away with her without his being able to say goodbye—or even watch. Decide for herself, she had said, but she would never come back, he knew that. Not when she came to a place where they were so wealthy and had everything. But she had decided to leave with them, otherwise she would have hidden somewhere. But maybe she was just playing along and wanted to have a look at them first.

The thought of it sent a flush of warmth through Larus, and he looked up at the sun as his restlessness grew. He might be able to make it. If he decided to go back now with the cows, maybe he could see them drive off with her—or see them have to leave without her. He thought hard. Was there anyone who would notice if he brought the cows back early on a day like this? If Tinka was able to get away with deciding so many things, then wasn't it only fair that he could decide something for once?

But at the same time he knew he wasn't put together the same way as Tinka; he was soft and timid inside, and because of that he would never dare spend one night in her shed in the grasslands. Still his legs started moving him around the cows and the shouts came out of his mouth all on their own like they usually did when it was time to go back. He didn't want to, at least that's what he thought. It just happened, and slowly he herded the obstinate animals together, who didn't think it was time yet.

When he was halfway home, he started speeding up. Now it was too late to change his mind; he had come too far to go back to the grasslands. It was now or never.

His hands were sweating when he realized he had gotten this far without having decided anything. He moaned silently to himself as he jogged along behind the trotting animals.

Through the village.

Through the gate.

And through the courtyard until they stopped at the closed barn door.

Larus stood there fiddling with the heavy iron hook which was binding in the latch when Master came rushing out to find out what was the matter, since he was back already. Larus shrank at the sound of Master's voice so close to him. He hadn't heard him come up and he turned with a start. Master was wearing his fine clothes, and behind him by the formal front door he saw the carriage. Larus lifted the latch and stepped aside so the cows could wander in on their own.

"Why are you back so early?" asked Master.

"Because—" Larus stopped. He was just about to say that it was because a wolf appeared, but then he gathered his courage and stood up straight.

"Well?" said Master.

"Because I have to say goodbye to Tinka," he said instead.

Master stared at the boy perplexed.

Then he just said, "What?" He was prepared for any kind of fabricated excuse and ready to respond with a box on the boy's ear. But the boy's straightforward answer took him by surprise.

Larus repeated that he had to say goodbye to Tinka, and Master shook his head in bewilderment and shuffled back to the front door. He had never heard anything like it—what was he supposed to say to that?

Meanwhile, a bit confused, Larus slipped into the barn, where he tied up the cows at their places and then stood by the window facing the courtyard. What was going to happen now? Was he not going to be punished until after they had driven off with her? It didn't really matter. After she was gone, nothing mattered anymore. He stood drawing on the small dirty panes with his finger while he waited for someone to go out to the horse barn and come out with the two unfamiliar horses which he knew must be in there. Master would do it, or maybe Master and the stranger together, since there was no grown-up farmhand here to do that kind of thing.

His finger stopped its path along the glass when the door across from him opened. Not the formal door like he had expected, but the scullery door they used every day. Tinka emerged in a red checkered dress with buttons and polished sandals. He had never seen her look so fine. If it weren't for her blonde hair sticking up, he would barely have recognized her. She looked around in every direction, and then she jogged over to the barn door, keeping an eye on the ground so she wouldn't step in chicken manure or other filth.

She wasn't used to wearing shoes, thought Larus, and definitely not ones like that. Then she pulled open the barn door and stood before him.

"I'm glad you showed up," she said quickly. "We're leaving soon."

We? thought Larus. Was she already thinking of them as we? She looked so strangely unfamiliar in those clothes.

"I just wanted to say goodbye to you," he said softly. "Are they nice?"

"I'm not really sure," said Tinka. He could hear hesitation in her voice. "They aren't sure that I'm the right one. I think they think that I don't look right. They keep looking at me in the strangest way and they want me to tell them my father's name."

"Did you tell them?" Larus had never heard her say anything about remembering her father's name.

Tinka shook her head calmly.

"But you know what it is?"

Tinka smiled delicately and secretively.

"Your mother was named Martha," said Larus.

"How do you know that?"

"Mistress and Master talked about it," he said.

"Plenty of people are named Martha," said Tinka.

"Aren't you going to tell them about your father?"

"They don't have to know every little thing. I want them to like me the way I am and not because my mother was their daughter."

"What did you say when they asked?"

"That I couldn't remember, of course."

"But you do know?" Larus was having trouble moving on from the subject. "You know, deep inside yourself, where the truth is?"

She looked in his eyes. Their eyes met, but she didn't answer.

"I want to give you a present," he said. "Something nice that you can take with you, but I don't have anything." "You shared your food with me back then when I was very hungry," she said. "I will always remember that."

Over at the farmhouse the formal front door opened and Master stepped out with the stranger who might be Tinka's grandfather. It was difficult to grasp. Larus stared at him as they walked over to the horse barn and each returned with a horse which they tied to the carriage. Then Mistress came outside with the wife, and Tinka said she had to leave now.

"I will come and visit you," she said, placing her hand gently on his arm.

"When?" he asked.

"I don't know—sometime."

Tinka left him standing there and walked out the door

and across the courtyard to where Mistress stood on the stoop. Mistress bent down over her and embraced her sadly. Larus could tell from where he stood.

Larus didn't go outside to wave. He didn't want anyone to see him as Tinka was being driven away. It hurt so much to stand at the window and see her step up into the fine carriage with the fine people in her fine clothes and roll out the gate. He didn't even go out to see which way they turned.

IX

Tinka was startled when the carriage started moving; she had never been in one before and didn't know the feeling. Her fingers grabbed firmly onto the front edge of the bench seat on both sides of her knees. Her eyes swam in her head because everything was moving past. The bumpy stones of Master's courtyard and all the buildings around it moved backwards. Nothing stood still anymore.

Tinka held on fast. Master and Mistress and the stoop on which they were standing glided past, then the windows of the farmhouse one by one and then the scullery door. Then the gate entrance thundered around them with the clatter of wheels and horseshoes, and the carriage crunched onto the gravel of the village road and turned left.

The man yelled to speed up the horses, and everything Tinka tried to focus on disappeared even faster behind them, leaving a dizzying feeling in her belly.

Why was it like this? Tinka had often seen carriages roll past on the street, and it appeared safe and easeful. She had never imagined it would feel different than it looked. Still she couldn't get rid of the uneasy feeling that she had lost her moorings; it stayed with her.

But she didn't say anything, not a word, not the least complaint, as she sat squeezed between two strangers who towered over her on either side. But her knuckles were white, her entire body felt white and taut, her teeth were clenched.

It was as if she had been captured. They took up too

much room next to her, and the musty smell of their seldom-used fine clothes irritated her nose and worsened her upset stomach. She was feeling sick.

Neither of the strangers said anything or looked at her as the trees and farms of the village flew past on both sides. Tinka wondered if maybe they were afraid she would change her mind and jump off or something like that. Or were they regretting this themselves? Were they sitting there wondering if she was actually their grandchild? While they were still inside Mistress's house they had eagerly tried to convince Tinka that they were truly her grandparents, and they smiled and were so friendly. And she had believed them when they said that they had had a daughter named Martha, and Tinka didn't refuse to go back with them. They told her she would be treated so well.

But now here she sat and didn't know what to believe. What if she threw up? Mistress would have noticed that she wasn't feeling well and would have asked if she was alright, but this big lady next to her just sat with her face forward just like the man on her other side. They didn't ask her anything.

But she was theirs now. They had bought her. Without a peep they had paid what Master required, while Mistress just stood out in the kitchen with her red teary eyes. Tinka felt a pang in her heart at the thought of Mistress, but Mistress wasn't her real family. Mistress never knew Tinka's mother.

When they were a good distance outside the village, the wife turned towards Tinka to say something, and Tinka hoped it was to ask how she was feeling. But the woman was thinking about something completely different.

"What was your mother's name?" she asked.

"Master told you," said Tinka.

"But I want to hear it from you. You do know, don't you?"

"Martha," said Tinka. She didn't think her mother resembled this heavy woman at all.

"You hear that, Herman? There you are," the woman exclaimed, rubbing her hands in her lap with satisfaction.

The husband just grunted. "Of course she's going to say that."

"What do you mean."

"What do you think she would say?" he said in the same tone of voice.

"But Herman—"

"Didn't we already tell what our daughter's name was—back when that farmhand asked, and now to these people? The more I think about it—"

Then no one spoke, and it gave Tinka the feeling that each of them were reliving what had been said at Master's house.

"But Herman, do you really think—?" the woman started to say, obviously in disbelief.

"You have always been so gullible," said the man. "Think about it for a second. Someone finds a girl who was abandoned out in the grasslands and brings her to the parish chairman. The girl doesn't want to go to the poorhouse, and no one in the parish wants to take her in. So what do you do? You try and find someone whose daughter ran away with a dirty rat day laborer and say here you go, here's your grandchild. Can't you see that?"

"Do you think I'm lying?" asked Tinka sharply.

"Who wouldn't lie in that situation?" growled the husband.

"But her name really was Martha," said Tinka.

"Well, it's too late now," said the man.

"If you don't believe what I say you can let me out right now," said Tinka. They had reached the area where Larus usually let the cows graze, and she could easily walk back herself.

"Oh, no. No way we're doing that. You're staying with us." said the man.

"But I don't want to live with anyone who thinks I'm lying," said Tinka, trying to stand up. But the man leaned over into her so she couldn't move.

"You forget that we paid for you. And you are going to work for that money," he said.

"But Herman, it could be that she is Martha's daughter," the woman whined.

"She could just as well be anyone else's. She doesn't look at all like Martha."

The wife bit her lip. "Do you think we should bring her back?"

"No," he said curtly.

"But if you really don't think she is Martha's? Then wouldn't that be best—we haven't gotten that far yet."

Tinka's ears perked up.

"No, now listen to me," said the man angrily.

Tinka sighed silently.

"Before we get too far?" said the wife.

"We are never going to get our money back," said the man. "And I am not going to let him keep the money and the girl. I have my limits."

His tone of voice gave Tinka the shivers.

They had arrived at a point where there wasn't a real road anymore, just ruts full of holes. The carriage body plunged and swung up and down and made Tinka's stomach hurt.

"I'm sick to my stomach," she whispered, feeling cold sweat on her forehead.

"Are you going to throw up?" The wife quickly picked up Tinka by the shoulders and held her out over the edge, just as Tinka's stomach turned over and made her whole lunch come up and out.

"Is there any more?" asked the woman, still holding her.

Tinka shook her head and felt her being placed back down between the adults. She wiped her forehead with her sleeve. That made her stomach feel a lot better, she thought, as her insides calmed down.

The wheel tracks led to the edge of a meadow, which turned into a real bog with black water holes and tall mounds with grass sticking out, resembling large heads with spiky hair bent at the tips. Tinka looked carefully at them. It seemed like a dangerous place, the kind of place her mother had warned her about when she was little.

She shuddered at the sight of all that dark, still water, and the wife looked down at her askance.

"Yes, now we're really out in the middle of nowhere," she said. "People don't live out here."

Tinka looked back in amazement. Evidently no one had ever told the woman that this was precisely where her own daughter had found a peaceful place to live, and that Tinka was living here until rather recently. Tinka sat there, feeling very much connected to her mother, but not at all in the same family as these two portly people she sat between, so she didn't say anything.

"What are you staring at," said the wife, irritated by Tinka's looking at her.

"You don't look at all like my mother," said Tinka, not averting her gaze.

The woman pursed her lips and turned her head to face straight ahead.

"Not even when she was lying there dead," continued Tinka.

"Don't get smart with me, little one," said the woman sharply. "That is no way to talk."

"Why not?"

"Because it is impudent."

"Even if it's true?"

"Hertha, stop talking to her and tell her to shut her mouth." The man's voice was mean, but he didn't turn his head or move a muscle.

"She has to learn how to behave," said the wife to diffuse the conflict. "She doesn't know anything."

"Well she'll learn—you can bet on that," said the man sternly.

Tinka shrank and went silent. It sounded like he meant it. She felt afraid and uncomfortable, and another thought occurred to her. Maybe they really were her mother's parents—and they were the ones who chased her out to the grasslands and let her stay there until she got sick and died. And her father too, but that was before. This idea rattled her, and she began to wonder how she could get away from them again and try to make it back to Mistress and Larus. She didn't think she could do it by herself; it was too far away.

She was afraid to say that she was hungry; she had thrown up her lunch. She knew there was a box under the driver's seat, but she didn't know if there was food inside it. The two grown-ups didn't look like they were lacking anything.

All she could do was try to fall asleep. She told herself she was a fox that had been trapped, so all she could do was to roll herself up with her tail over her nose and wait. She held onto this image until she fell asleep.

She woke up when the carriage came to a stop. Carefully she opened her eyes halfway and tried to see where she was, but when the woman stood up to get out, Tinka quickly closed her eyes again.

"Pick her up," said the wife. And the husband took hold of Tinka and held her upright on the seat until the woman was standing on the ground to receive Tinka in her arms. Tinka glimpsed a farm courtyard as she was carried around the carriage and into a house. And then on through a foyer into a drawing room. Here she was placed down on a chair. Two young women entered from the opposite side and came over to get a look at the new arrival.

It lasted a long time. So long that Tinka felt a distancing on their part. They examined her in silence and they did not look too pleased. On the contrary, they seemed disappointed in the way she looked.

Finally one of them opened her mouth.

"She doesn't look like Martha," she said reproachfully, as if the child had a flaw. "She doesn't look like her at all."

Not even a hello or a welcome, thought Tinka, staring

back at them as hard as she could. They must be Martha's sisters, her mother's sisters; they had the same dark features. But what did they expect? That their runaway sister was going to come back in a younger replica?

"She looks pretty spindly to me," said the other one. "How old did you say she was supposed to be?" She turned to face her mother.

"Eight," said the woman.

Tinka thought to herself: nine. She was sure she had turned nine since Larus found her.

"But do you think that's really the case?" she asked doubtfully.

"That's what she said herself," answered the woman.

"I figured as much. She's probably lying."

Tinka glared offended at the young woman. How could she know? Why didn't they just ask her?

Instead they stood there looking at her, talking over her like she was a pig or a calf they had bought at market. Then they were quiet for a short while.

Then the first sister said, "Do you really think she could be Martha's daughter?"

"She said herself that that was her mother's name," said the wife in a tired voice.

"Then that's probably a lie too. Someone told her to say that."

"That's what your father said," sighed the woman.

"Why in the world did you bring her back with you?"

"Because we had gone all that way and your father had paid them what they wanted."

"Paid? You didn't tell us that you paid money for her." The daughter stared at her mother with obvious indignation.

"They wanted compensation for all the time they had put her up," said the mother, almost apologetically.

Then it got quiet again.

"And that hair," said the first daughter again. "Quite a spectacle. Not from anyone in our family anyway."

"But maybe the father's," said the mother softly.

The aunts thought it over.

"But wasn't he rather blonde?" asked the mother, when they didn't say anything.

"Red-haired," they said simultaneously.

That gave Tinka a start. Then they really were her family. The two old people were her grandparents and the two younger ones her aunts. Tinka's father had had red hair, bright red. But why didn't they seem happy to see her at all? And why wouldn't they talk to her?

"They're all red-haired in that family," said one of the aunts.

Like an insult, thought Tinka. Evidently none of them liked red hair.

"Can she talk?" asked the other aunt.

"Why wouldn't she be able to talk?" said their father. "We did find out that she had been living alone like a wild animal. Wasn't that what he said, the parish chairman's farmhand?"

"She was talking fine there where we got her," said the wife.

"So maybe she's still kind of wild?" said the other aunt, inspecting Tinka who was sitting motionless on the chair.

"Not that I've noticed," said the woman. "Her Mistress was able to call for her, in from outside, too. Otherwise we wouldn't have brought her back with us."

Tinka sat there feeling more and more uncomfortable. Why didn't they just ask her instead of thinking she was like an ignorant animal? But maybe they didn't think she could understand what they were saying. Her mother and father were not wild animals. They taught her how to behave properly a long time ago.

"So what is her name?" asked the aunts.

"Tinka," said the wife. "At least that's what the people said where we got her."

"Tinka? No one in our family ever had that name," blurted out one of the aunts.

Tinka looked down at the floor and thought that her mother didn't want to name her child for anyone in the family that had forced her to run away. It was quiet for a while as they wondered where her name had come from.

"Maybe it's not a real name," said one of the aunts.

"Maybe she doesn't know her own name."

"Or maybe she was named after the old woman who ended up down at the bog," said the other aunt. "The father's mother. I'm pretty sure her name was Katinka."

It looked like the name Katinka gave them a bad taste in their mouths. As if it had just struck them that through Martha's child they were now connected by family to someone they absolutely did not want to be in the same family with.

"You can't baptize a child with that name," said the one aunt.

"Do you think she was even baptized?" said the other. "How could she be?"

They looked at one another.

"We could change that pretty easily," said the first one.

"Right, if we're going to keep her," said the other.

The aunt's 'if' jangled through Tinka's body. They didn't even know if they wanted her to stay. And in any case they were not going to take away her name. If her mother knew how important it was to sing at her father's burial, then she must also have known how important it was to baptize her child. And she did it herself, just like she buried her husband when he died. Tinka was certain she had been baptized, even though it was never written down in any church record.

The one aunt asked her, "What is your real name?"

"Tinka," she said.

"No, really. Your real name."

"Tinka," she said again.

"No, not that awful name. That's not a real name."

"At least not in this house," added the other aunt. "It would have looked better for Martha if she had called her child after someone in her own family, and not after—one of them. That could be a big problem. What are we going to do with her? Why did you bring her back with you?" She turned accusingly towards her mother.

"But we were under the impression that she was Martha's daughter," said the wife.

"And what proof do we have of that?" asked the one aunt.

"And if she is, then she's also Thormod's daughter," said the other aunt. "And I don't see why we should be raising his kids."

It startled Tinka to hear her father's name said aloud, but she tried not to show it. She looked from one woman to the other, and it became easier for her to understand why her mother had to run away from her childhood home. Why she preferred living in the deserted woods hungry and poor instead of staying in her village. Their influence must have been excessive back then too, and she would never have been allowed to marry the man she loved.

Tinka decided right then that she wasn't going to stay either. Not that she really knew how she was going to make it back to Mistress, but she could try to behave such that they would send her back of their own accord. The husband had said they couldn't do that because they had paid for her, and she should earn back the money. Tinka thought he meant that she should be their servant girl.

But at dinnertime she found out there already was a maid, a girl nearly grown, who didn't sit with them at the table. She carried in the bowls and plates and placed them in front of the wife, and each time she stole a glance at Tinka.

The room was very quiet. Tinka didn't know if it was always this quiet when they ate, or if it was because of her. The old woman who had brought her back put food on Tinka's plate and placed it in front of her. But Tinka didn't start eating. For a long time she sat there waiting to be able to eat in peace. She was very hungry, but they were all staring at her.

Tinka thought it was because they wanted to see if she had good manners or if she devoured her food like an animal. She could do it either way. But she was sure that even if they appeared to want her to eat nicely, deep down they really wanted the opposite. Something dramatic. That was why they were sitting there watching her, even though they were pretending not to.

Tinka decided to do her worst, so they could come to a quick decision and send her back.

It was hot food. Gravy and potatoes and meat. They probably hadn't figured on getting served hot food in the middle of the day at Mistress's house, or maybe they always ate hot food in the evening. Maybe they thought that was more high-class.

"Eat," said the wife for the third time. She probably thought Tinka was being picky. All the others were still looking at Tinka.

Tinka picked up a potato in each hand and pushed them around in the gravy. Then she stuffed them in her mouth as if she hadn't had anything to eat for several days. Then she did the same with the meat. It was hot in her hands, but the food had already sat on the plate for a while, so it wasn't burning hot.

A gasp of exasperation traveled around the table among the others. They forgot to eat anything themselves. All they did was stare at Tinka without saying a word, until she picked up her plate and licked it clean.

"Why don't you do something!" the husband said to his wife from the head of the table. His face was red with anger.

"What do you want me to do?" said the wife. "You saw yourself at lunch that she ate with a fork and knife." "That is no way to eat, to play with the food like that," he continued. "If she was our daughter I would slap her."

Tinka put her plate back down on the tablecloth. She had gravy on her hands and in her bangs and on her nose and her chin. What her grandfather meant was that she was so far removed from his family that he couldn't even hit her when she did something wrong.

But the wife took a towel and leaned over and roughly wiped off the sharp features of Tinka's little face.

"That was the animal in her coming out," hissed one aunt through her teeth.

"What animal?" said the husband from the head of the table, who hadn't heard what had been discussed before the meal.

"Like an animal," said the aunt. "It comes from living in the wild and not being around other people."

"A wolf," said Tinka, looking over at the man's face.

"What wolf?" He squinted his eyes at her.

"Me," she said. "Once I bit a fox."

"Hogwash," he said.

"But it's true. I did."

"Right, sure you did," he grumbled. "Do not talk back, at least not in this house."

Tinka pursed her mouth shut without shifting her gaze from him.

Then the maid came in with a large bowl of fruit compote and a stack of bowls which she placed in front of the lady of the house. And the husband glared threateningly from the head of the table when a plate of compote with milk was placed in front of Tinka.

She could see that he was keeping an eye on her, and that he was already mad. Still she picked up the plate with both hands and put it to her lips and started to slurp the contents down while looking at him over the edge of the plate.

The man's anger flared and he shouted that she was doing it on purpose. That this was clear and simple obstinance.

"Put the plate back down," he demanded.

But Tinka didn't put it down. She kept on sucking on the sweet compote and milk mixture.

He jumped up and marched angrily around the table, grabbed Tinka firmly by the arm and pulled her up out of her chair.

"If you are going to live here with us you have to behave properly," he roared. Everyone else around the table sat motionless.

It hurt her arm, as Tinka could barely reach the floor. Hanging from her one arm, she let the rest of the compote slide off the edge of the plate as he shook her. When the plate was empty she let go of it and it shattered against the floor.

"Look at that," she said.

There was red fruit compote in blotches all down the front of her dress. The man pushed her away from him in disgust, so firmly that Tinka fell to the floor on the other side of the chair.

"But Herman—" said the wife, rising from her chair.

"Don't bother defending her," he shouted. "She was doing it all on purpose."

Then he walked out and slammed the door.

"Now get up," said the wife. She was angry now.

Tinka slowly stood up and started to unbutton her dress.

"What are you doing now?"

"Taking it off," said Tinka.

"Not here."

"But it's all wet." Tinka let the stained dress fall down around her and stepped out of it.

"Can't you see we're eating?" said the wife.

"Yes," said Tinka, standing behind her chair.

The wife looked at her with resignation.

"Then sit back down, at least," she sighed.

"No," said Tinka. "It's all over the chair, too."

"How disgusting," said one aunt.

"What else did you expect?" said the other. "I don't see how anyone could think this was Martha's daughter—with those manners," said the first aunt.

"I think you're wrong," said her sister. "That's why this is Martha's daughter—with those manners. She would have reacted the same way. Don't you see that?"

Right after the meal the wife led Tinka into the guest room and put her to bed.

X

Even though the doors were closed, Tinka could hear voices coming from somewhere. Loud excited voices reached her in the dark. It was late, but they hadn't gone to bed.

Tinka couldn't make out what they were talking about, not even if she moved the blanket away from her ears, but she was sure that she was the cause of the upset. To them she was a wild thing, a creature who hadn't received proper discipline and upbringing. They were convinced she would cause them trouble and be an inconvenience, and she had no doubt they were about to decide to drive her back where they got her. Tinka snuggled satisfied in the strange bed.

When she woke up again it was light out, but the house was silent. Tinka didn't know how early or late it was, and she quietly crawled out of bed and looked around for the bundle of clothes Mistress had sent along with her, but she couldn't find it anywhere. She only had her underclothes.

Cautiously she opened her door. The hall was empty. An entire night had passed since she had heard the raised voices. She walked slowly and carefully to the kitchen where the woman sat alone at the table with a cup of coffee in front of her.

"So there you are finally," she said. "The morning is half over."

"I can't find my clothes," said Tinka.

139

The old woman pointed tiredly at the bundle, which was still lying on the countertop by the door.

"Why did you misbehave last night?" she asked.

"Because I ended up in the wrong place," said Tinka, picking up the bundle. "I want to go home now."

"That was dumb of you," said the woman.

"Why?" Tinka opened the bundle and took out one of her old dresses. She noticed the new red checkered dress was hanging on the string above the stove. Someone had washed it.

"What do you mean 'the wrong place'?" asked the woman, while Tinka got dressed.

"Because there's no one here who likes me," said Tinka. "I thought you were like my mother, but you aren't like her at all. No one here is like her."

"But you are like her," said the woman.

"Yesterday you all said I was like my father," said Tinka.

"The way you look maybe, but you are just as obstinate as Martha." The woman stood up and scooped out a glob of warm porridge onto a plate from a large pot which was still on the stove. Tinka figured it was left over from breakfast.

"And if you throw this on the floor, you aren't getting anything else," said the woman soberly as she poured milk on top.

"I didn't spill the compote," said Tinka flatly. "If he hadn't yanked my arm it wouldn't have happened."

"He is your grandfather."

"Right," said Tinka. "He is the one who forced my mother to leave home."

"She could have just done as we said. Plenty of others would have married her. She could have had a decent husband."

"My father was a decent husband," said Tinka.

"Your father was a poor louse," said the woman bitterly. "What did he have to offer her?"

"Himself," said Tinka. "He loved her and she loved him. They were happy to be together."

Tinka sat down at the table and started to eat her porridge. "They sang," she said softly.

"Sang?" The woman turned with a doubting smirk.

"Yes, they sang to each other when they were working. And sometimes they cried—together."

"Out of misery," said the woman, "because she couldn't stay away from him. And what did she get out of it? What did she get out of it? Tell me that."

"Me," said Tinka, between spoonfuls.

"Right, God help me."

No one spoke for a while after that.

"Do you ever sing?" asked Tinka.

"Never," said the woman dismissively.

"Not even when you're alone—to yourself?"

"Why would I do that? Do you think I have a reason to sing?" Her voice was bitter, thought Tinka.

"But you have everything, don't you?" asked Tinka.

"What everything?" The woman stood up and felt Tinka's dress to see if was nearly dry.

"All the things," said Tinka. "A big fine house with everything you could want inside, a proper, right kind of husband with lots of money and two daughters who do what you tell them—why shouldn't you sing?" The woman went stock-still where she was standing and stared at Tinka while her one arm hung in the dress over the stove. Then her face became darker suddenly.

"Now you are just being smart-mouthed, little lady. You don't know what you're talking about. Eat your food." The woman's voice was stern, but Tinka was not to be stopped.

"My mother wouldn't trade," she said. "She would rather live alone and be poor and sometimes not have anything to eat—as long as she could decide for herself."

"That was your father's influence. He lured her out there."

"Then why didn't she move back here after she buried him?"

"Buried? What do you mean?"

"Out there—in the ground."

The woman's eyes widened with horror. "What are you saying?"

"That she buried him in the ground after he died," said Tinka very clearly.

"All by herself?"

"Who else was going to do it? When you live in a place like that you have to do everything yourself."

"I thought they had some kind of connection to his family—your father's." The woman looked down at her hands and spoke softly. "That's what I always thought—"

"Not after he got sick. He couldn't walk the long distance."

"What did he die from?" The woman was still speaking softly.

"A sore on his foot—it wouldn't heal—in the end his whole leg turned black."

"You saw it?"

"I stood there when she washed him."

"How disgusting." The old woman wrung her hands with revulsion.

"I saw when she buried him too. She sang a different kind of song then."

The woman at the table got a strange helpless look in her large droopy face.

"So she could have come back then," she mumbled to herself.

"Right," said Tinka. "But she didn't want to."

The woman sighed.

"I think I know why she didn't want to," said Tinka.

"And why is that?"

"For the same reason I don't want to be here." Tinka pushed away the empty plate.

"And where do you want to go?" asked the woman, her voice taking a hard tone again.

"Where you got me."

"Well that is not up to you to decide," said the woman. "And besides, they don't want you."

"Mistress does."

"Then why did they sell you?"

"Because Master is a proper, decent man. He made money from it."

They heard tramping of clogs out in the front court-yard, and the sound of horseshoes and carriage wheels. Tinka felt warm inside. They were probably going to drive her back this very day.

"If you are done eating then wipe your mouth," said the woman after a quick glance outside.

Tinka quickly took the towel and did as she was told. Then, to the woman's amazement, Tinka carried her dish to the sink. Then the husband opened the door and stood in the open doorway.

"Well?" he said.

"Yes," said his wife, getting up from her chair and taking down Tinka's red-checkered dress from the string. She folded it and tucked it into the bundle which Tinka had left open. Then she re-tied its corners.

"So are you going to drive me home after all?" asked Tinka carefully, turning towards the man in the doorway.

He hesitated a moment.

"You could call it that," he said. "Are you coming?" Tinka walked over to the woman and reached out her hand and curtseyed as Mistress had taught her. Then she picked up her bundle and followed the man out to the courtyard. Afterwards she wondered if she should have just left, since no one had greeted her the previous day.

It was a different horse and a different kind of carriage than the day before. The carriage was much smaller and only had two wheels. The horse wasn't very big either. Tinka was disappointed at the sight. Could a flimsy vehicle like that handle the rough and bumpy track back to Mistress's house? She didn't think it looked very reassuring. Maybe it was because the wife wasn't going to come, she thought, stepping up hesitantly onto the step and sitting down on the little bench seat on the one side. The wagon tipped dangerously when the man got in after her and sat on the other side facing her, and the horse uneasily shifted its hooves.

Then they drove off, and the wife reluctantly lifted her

hand halfway in a kind of wave, and let it fall again. Tinka was occupied with holding on. The little wagon followed the horse's movements very differently than the large four-wheeled carriage from the day before.

They drove through the village, but instead of staying on the road they turned off, and Tinka got the impression they were driving down and around behind the farms and away from them. She didn't dare ask if this was the same way they had come the previous day; she had slept through the last part of the trip. They kept driving slightly downhill, and after a long distance black water pits appeared in between strips of grass where peat was laid to dry. She could see that this was a bog, a peat bog.

But there were people living here. There were small crooked houses along the road, and to her surprise there were some little children playing. It looked like a tiny and very poor village, well-hidden from the road with the large farms. Tinka looked around in wonder.

At the sight of the carriage, the children stopped playing and ran clinging to some women washing clothes at a little stream. Here they huddled together, staring perplexed at the strangers.

The women straightened their backs, with wet articles of clothing in their hands and mistrusting expressions on their faces. A wealthy farmer from the village was not usually a good sign, and it was obvious they expected bad news. They did not approach the newcomers.

The man stopped the horse next to the women washing and he shouted for Katinka.

They stared at him for a moment, before one of the women slowly stepped forward from the others and neared the carriage.

"That's my mother," she said. "What do you want her for?"

"To speak to her."

"My mother is old," said the woman. "What do want with her?"

"To speak to her, I told you. I bring a greeting." The woman's eye glanced at the child in the carriage without closer examination. And Tinka couldn't help but feel a certain discomfort in the woman, who straightened the scarf wound tightly around her head and smoothed the front of her wet dress. Then she reached out and gave the dripping laundry she had in her hand back to one of the others.

"I can take you over there," she said, turning and walking barefoot. The horse followed alongside her to one of the poorly maintained houses.

"Wait here," she said, and she went inside.

It took a good while before she reappeared with a stooped old woman who walked with two canes. The daughter led the old woman to a tree trunk where she could sit down.

"Are you Katinka?" asked the man in the carriage.

The old woman turned her wrinkled and furrowed face anxiously towards her daughter.

"What did he say?" she asked.

"He's asking if you are Katinka," she repeated in a loud, clear voice.

The old woman nodded. "Yes," she said. "That's me."

"Then I have a granddaughter for you," said the man in the carriage, in a voice tinged with gloating.

The old woman looked up at her daughter again. "What did he say there?" she asked.

"That he has a granddaughter for you," said the daughter.

Tinka sat stiff as a rail staring from one to the other, from the old woman's wrinkled face to the younger woman's mouth which just had the hint of a few lines. So this was—this was—

"What do you mean granddaughter?" said the old woman dismissively. "We're not missing anyone."

"This is Thormod's bastard child," said the man in the carriage.

It gave Tinka a start to hear her father's name, and she saw it had the same effect on the old woman's daughter.

"Thormod? But Thormod—" The woman didn't know what to say.

"What did he say?" asked the old woman.

"That it's Thormod's daughter," said the daughter. She wrinkled her brow with curiosity.

"Get down," the man said to Tinka.

Tinka didn't move. He couldn't just let her out here. She was going back to Mistress.

"Get down, I said!" he roared in her face, and Tinka jumped up and nearly fell out of the carriage and down onto the ground.

Then the young woman asked, "How could she be Thormod's girl? We haven't heard from him in years."

Tinka stood up with her bundle in her hand in front of the two women who were staring at her skeptically.

"You can ask her yourself. Someone found her out in the grasslands in the area where he lived," said the man.

"That doesn't make her his daughter," said the woman.

"She's Katinka's granddaughter," said the man, this

time loud enough so the old woman understood him. And she raised her trembling head towards the well-dressed farmer who gave no intention of getting down from his carriage.

"She is just as much your granddaughter," she shouted back at him. "You can take her back with you; we have plenty out here."

Her voice cracked with the strain and ended with a violent coughing attack.

"Martha has not been my daughter, not since Thormod lured her away," shouted the man. Then he turned back to his horse and quickly drove away.

And there stood Tinka. Alone, in front of two upset women, she got scared and started to run after the the small carriage which had brought her there. But the man set the horse to galloping and she had to give up. But he was her grandfather; he couldn't just abandon her here with people she didn't even know. She lay down in the wheel track and sobbed as Katinka's daughter walked over to her.

"Why are you crying?" asked the woman.

"I thought he was going to drive me home to Mistress," sobbed Tinka.

"What Mistress? Come over to the stream and tell us what kind of a mess you are in. Why did Herman come and drop you off here? He must know that we barely have enough to eat." She picked up Tinka from the wheel track and led her over to the washing area.

"What's your name?" the woman asked.

"Tinka."

That gave the woman a start. "That is what they called

my mother when she was a little girl. But no one calls her that anymore. How did you get that name?"

"I don't know. That's what my mother and father called me."

"Then is it true that you are Thormod's daughter?"

"Well, that was my father's name," whispered Tinka, "and my mother's name was Martha. But they both died. That was a long time ago."

The woman went silent and bit her lip.

"Do you remember the way he looked, your father?" she asked.

"He had red hair, with freckles on his face, and on his arms and his back in the summer."

The four women looked at one another over Tinka's head, a long, telling look that was heavy with something almost like a sigh. Tinka couldn't help but feel that she would be a burden if she stayed here, since they barely had enough food already.

The woman asked her, "But if you are Martha Enegård's daughter, then why would her father bring you down here to the bog?"

"They didn't like me. None of them liked me. They said I looked like my father's family and that I wasn't raised properly. And the wife said I was just as obstinate as my mother."

"That sounds like revenge, to drop her off here. He's taking revenge on us because he can't get to Thormod," said one of the other women.

"I thought he was going to drive me back to Mistress's farm," said Tinka softly.

"What Mistress are you talking about?"

"Where Larus works."

"And who is Larus?"

"He brings their cows out and tends them in the grass-lands."

"A hired boy?"

"Yes."

Tinka started to tell how she had found Larus and how he had shared his food with her, and how he had coerced her into coming back with him to the farm. And she told about Mistress, who tried to leave her at the poorhouse, and how she ran away and hid in Larus's room, and how it all ended up.

The other women forgot their laundry while they listened, and the little children who kept their distance from the strange girl at first, now filtered closer, until they were standing right next to Tinka, staring at her face with big round eyes.

"So you say that Mistress liked you in the end?" asked one of the other women.

"I am pretty sure she wanted to keep me as her own daughter," said Tinka.

"Well then why did she send you away?"

"It wasn't her, it was Master. When he heard that the parish chairman had found some of my mother's family, and that they were rich, then he wanted money for having kept me in their house."

"Did he get money?"

"He said he did."

"How much?"

"I don't know, but enough that the man who was supposed to be my grandfather felt like it was a lot and resented me for it."

"Hmm. But he must have plenty of money to keep you around," said the one who must have been Tinka's aunt.

Tinka shrugged. "I didn't want to stay there anyway," she said. "They weren't like the family I had imagined. None of them were like my mother in the least. Not one of them even talked to me or asked me anything. They talked around me like I was deaf, like I was some kind of strange animal."

"And what did you do?"

"I acted like a strange animal, of course. I ate with my fingers like I didn't know what a fork was, and I stuck my head down on my plate and licked up the gravy."

A wave of laughter spread around the four women, and their faces became milder.

"Oh, god, I would have loved to have seen that!" exclaimed Tinka's aunt.

"It got bad when we came to fruit compote for dessert and I did the same thing. Then he got so angry that he rushed over to my chair and yanked me out of it so I was just about hanging from my elbow, and he held me there while all the compote and milk ran down my dress and onto the chair and everywhere."

"Oh, my heavens. That you dared to do such a thing. Did he hit you?"

"No, he threw me down on the floor and walked out and slammed the door. But I was just doing that so he would drive me back to Mistress's house."

"Then what happened?"

"The wife got mad and put me to bed. And then they brought me here."

"What do you think will happen now?"

"I don't know. I wish I could go back home—to Mistress."

"But do you think she will take you in? And really keep you?"

"I know that she was crying when they drove me away."

"Why did you go with them?"

"Because I thought someone in their family would be like my mother."

"What if you could find someone here who was like your father?"

"I know you don't have enough food to let me stay here," whispered Tinka, looking down at the ground.

"I'm your father's sister," said the woman who was talking the most.

"Yes," said Tinka, but she didn't think it was right to ask if she could stay with her.

The woman lifted her arms and untied the knot in her tight headscarf, so her copper-colored hair was visible. And inside Tinka something curled up painfully. She had never seen anyone with such bright red hair since her father died.

Tinka looked at her but had trouble seeing her with all the tears suddenly filling up her eyes.

"Do you believe me?" asked her aunt.

Tinka nodded, overwhelmed.

"You probably shouldn't expect too much from your mother's family," said the aunt, "but you should know that two of your father's brothers live here, besides your grandmother and me. Both your uncles are day-laborers, but when they come home tonight we can talk to them about how to get you transportation back to this Mistress you talk about. If she really wants you, can she give you a better life than we can here? We have to send our children out to work by the time they are seven," she added with a sigh. "But I still want you to know that you can always come back to us if you have no other place to go."

"Thank you," whispered Tinka, not knowing what else to say.

"You can earn a serving of potatoes for tonight if you will watch these children and keep them away from the stream so we can finish washing our clothes before the men come home," said the aunt, walking back into the water.

XI

While they ate, Tinka had a hard time taking her eyes off of the two uncles because they looked so much like her father. But they were different too. They talked a lot and the same way he did, and they laughed like he did, but still they weren't him. It was strange.

They ate together in the largest of the houses so all of them could be together and talk. The smallest of the children had to sit on laps of the adults so they could all fit around the table. And extra plates and forks had to be borrowed from the other houses. Tinka's arrival was evidently something which affected the entire family.

They tried to put their heads together to figure out which village Tinka had come from. Tinka had to explain and explain, both how the village looked and what it was called and what the names were of the people who lived there, and how the church looked, if it was red brick or whitewashed. But the village was so far away that no one there was familiar with it.

"It's on the other side of where my mother and father lived," said Tinka.

They nodded, even though they didn't know much about the area over there.

Then they started to ask her what it was like where she lived, and if her parents had had a good life, and if her mother had done alright after her father died, and how she survived after her mother died too. It was quiet around the table as Tinka told her story. Someone placed potatoes on her plate, and after she was done peeling them, someone else poured melted fat on them from the pan. But it was a long while before she was finished talking so she could start to eat.

"I was there one time," said one uncle, "and it was the night I drove them out there. In the back of the wagon they had the few household items they had accumulated, and as many tools and implements as we could spare from around here. They also had their bedding and two old horse blankets to sleep under until they got their house built. Later it was always your father who came here if they needed something, and we helped him as much as we could, but I was only there that one time, and that was a long time ago. But I can try to find it again if that would be any help. I just don't know how to get from the village out to where they were."

"But I know how to do that," shouted Tinka. Her heart did a somersault at the thought of it.

"Then we'll have to see if we can borrow a cart," said one of the others. "Does anyone know someone with a tumbrel they're not using at the moment?" Tinka could see they were all thinking. "What is a tumbrel?" she said.

"A work cart," someone answered.

"The kind you use in the fields," said another.

Tinka nodded. She knew what they were.

"They don't go very fast," said the uncle. "So it will probably take twice as long as a carriage. They're not very comfortable either, but it's the only way."

"If my mother and father could use one to get there, then I can too," said Tinka. "When do you think you can borrow it?" she said.

"Maybe on Sunday. We're going to need a horse too."

"Not until Sunday?" Tinka had hoped that maybe they could leave the next day. The others could see that she was disappointed.

"You have to understand that day-laborers don't get to decide over when they can do things," explained her aunt. "There is only a day off on Sunday, and even that's not always the case."

"I see," said Tinka, embarrassed that she hadn't thought of that.

"And you will have to wake up so early in the morning it will still be partly night, if Manfred is going to be able to make it back on the same day."

"I see," whispered TInka, realizing that she would have to stay in this place for almost an entire week.

Tinka ended up sleeping in her grandmother's kitchen trunk, which also served as a bench. The old woman said that no one else was sleeping in it these days. Otherwise there were often periods when a couple of grandchildren slept there when there wasn't room at their own houses. But now the older ones had been hired out.

So that was why there were only little children around the area, thought Tinka. She watched her grandmother remove the lid and fluff up the straw.

"We don't even have to pull it out," said the old woman. "You don't take up much room." She waited while Tinka pulled off her dress and set her fine sandals aside. A cloth blanket made of woolen squares sewn together was placed over her and she quickly fell asleep.

The ensuing days went by much more quickly than

Tinka had imagined they would. There was always something she could help with, and not only watching over the small children. She ground grain, she picked blueberries and cowberries in the low hills beside the bog, she gathered eggs from the free-roaming chickens who made nests under bushes and other strange places, and she helped with weeding various gardens. And the whole time she learned new things which she hadn't learned at Mistress's house.

But if the farmer from Enegård thought he could beat Tinka down by leaving her in a poor settlement, he was wrong. There was no one here by the bog as poor as her parents had been in their deserted homestead, and definitely not as poor Tinka was when she was alone after they died. Tinka thought a lot about this during the week.

The day she arrived, one of the women said that he was trying to get revenge on her father's family. That was probably right. The farmer from Enegård could never accept that one of his daughters opposed him and demanded control over her own life—and all this due to a day-laborer.

The demeaning tone in which her father and his family had been discussed in town had undeniably given them a bad reputation compared to the farmers. But Tinka felt much more comfortable here, down in the bog, than up there among the fine people. In comparison to her parents, Mistress and Master had been dizzyingly rich, but compared to the family at Enegård, Master was not worth very much.

Tinka also wondered if her grandfather was seeking revenge against Master by bringing her here, instead of bringing her back. Her grandfather had said in the carriage that there was no way Master was going to keep both the money and her.

And besides this, Tinka was sure that her grandfather was also getting back at her, because just like her mother, she wouldn't do as he said. So he abandoned her in the most miserable place he could imagine—and he had no idea how nice it had been for her, apart from there not being a lot to eat. Here there were people to talk with, and she was a part of everything that happened. If they had the means to keep her, and if it hadn't been for Mistress, then she would have liked to have stayed. But it wouldn't be fair for them to send their own children off to work when they were seven, and then take her in and feed her when she was nine.

Also, if you were one of the people by the bog there were a lot of things you couldn't do. For example, you couldn't own land. Not even if they had enough money to buy some, they would not be allowed. It was barely tolerated that they had dug small beds at the foot of the hill where they raised cabbages and potatoes. Tinka's grandmother told her that.

They weren't allowed to dig peat either, her grandmother said, because they didn't own the bog. But when the farmhands from town drove away, they were permitted to gather up the pieces that were left behind on the ground.

They weren't allowed to have cows either, because they weren't able to feed them, since they didn't have their own land. But they circumvented this somewhat by having two goats who were on tethers at the edge of the bog. In the summer when the weather was hot, the women cut branches from the willows and dried them for winter fodder. Tinka listened to her grandmother with great interest.

"And it is also forbidden to fish in the stream," said her grandmother.

"Are there fish in it?" asked Tinka surprised.

"Both trout and eels," said her grandmother.

"Lots of farmers have traps in the water down here."

"Why can't you put a trap out too?" asked Tinka.

"They won't let us, and if they find one they destroy it," said the old woman.

Tinka could easily imagine the farmer from Enegård trampling a trap he had pulled out of the water.

"But sometimes we have eel anyway," said the old woman with a sly laugh.

"How do you get them? Do you take them from the other traps?"

"Never," snapped her grandmother sternly. "We never touch any of their traps. That would be very dangerous."

"Then how?"

"We crochet them," said the old woman in her sly voice.

Tinka looked at her confused. She didn't know what that meant.

"We collect earthworms when they come up out of the ground at night. A lot of worms, several pails full," said her grandmother.

"Do you eat them instead?" asked Tinka, remembering what she had survived on back with her chickens.

"No!" shouted the old woman with revulsion.

"But they are easy to chew," said Tinka.

"Stop that. No one eats earthworms," said her grandmother. "Just the thought of it."

"But I used to," said Tinka. "Back when all I had were the chickens, they taught me how."

Her grandmother looked at her hard and said, "Are you teasing me? Or is that true?"

"It's true," said Tinka a bit offended. "Why else would I say it?"

"But if you had chickens, why didn't you eat them?"

"There were only two of them. And then I would have been alone and I wouldn't have had them to talk to."

"Oh, my poor child—that you were in such a bad way," sighed the old woman, pulling Tinka close. "That Thormod's little girl had to survive by eating worms." For a while it was quiet between them.

Then Tinka returned to her grandmother's story and asked, "So what did you do with all the worms you collected?"

"We sewed them together," said the old woman.

"Sewed them?" asked Tinka. "How?"

"With a needle and thread, and they wound together into a clump."

"That sounds disgusting," said Tinka.

"And then we would tie a piece of fishing line to the clump, and when the nights were dark and warm, we would sit by the stream holding our bait in the water." Tinka stared at her without saying a word.

"And when the eels came by to gnaw on the worms, their teeth got stuck in the thread, and we would lift them out of the water and put them in the sack. That is the only way we catch eels."

Tinka was still quiet.

Noticing Tinka's silence, her grandmother asked, "What are you thinking about?"

"Wasn't that a shame for the worms?" she asked. "To be sewn together like that?"

"Is that worse than chewing them with your teeth?" asked her grandmother.

Tinka didn't know how to answer that.

"In both cases it was to stay alive," said the old woman. "We eat the eels of course."

The old woman had trouble walking. Her back was sore and she couldn't stand up straight, so she had to walk bent over, supported by two canes. This is why she could no longer work, unless it was something she could do sitting down. She could sew and knit and clean cabbages and things like that. When Tinka didn't have anything else to do, she went and sat with the old woman and got her to tell stories about the people in the village or about the old days, or about ghosts and trolls out in the bog. At times when Tinka had to watch the children while the adult women were busy, she liked to bring them with her over to her grandmother. They would sit still until one of them peed their pants and had to be tended to.

The week flew by for Tinka, and before she knew it, it was Sunday, and she had to wake up early. The uncle who was going to drive her had already left for the village to go get the horse and cart he had permission to use. His name was Manfred. And when he returned, all the people from the bog crowded around to say goodbye to Tinka. Both her aunts assured her that she could come back if she weren't allowed to stay with Mistress.

Tinka was speechless. She just stood there drawing in the dirt with the toe of her shoe. Suddenly she bent down and took off her sandals, and then she opened her bundle and took out the nice red-checkered dress. She handed them to her old grandmother who had taken care of her.

"This is for letting me stay here," she said weakly.

They all protested and said that she didn't have to pay to stay with them.

"It's not a payment," said Tinka. "Not really. I would rather go barefoot, and that dress will always remind me of my grandfather who didn't want me."

"She hung the dress over the shoulders of her bent grandmother, and placed the shoes next to her canes. Then she turned around and quickly crawled up into the cart.

"When I get big I will come back and visit you," she said.

They smiled at her doubtfully.

Then her uncle Manfred climbed up in the cart and sat on the narrow driver's bench next to Tinka. He shouted a command to the horse and the animal plodded down the dirt path up towards the village.

This time nothing was going by dizzyingly, thought Tinka. The cart was stiff, and it bumped and bounced along the uneven tracks. Still she was in a good mood. This was the way back to Mistress; she was on her way home. Her bundle lay behind her, and in her lap she held a small cloth with a bit of bread and a couple of apples for them to eat along the way. That was what they could spare from the small sunken houses at the edge of the bog.

At first, Tinka talked non-stop. There was no one awake yet in the village as they drove through, and she asked about all kinds of things. She was brimming with anticipation, and Uncle Manfred did his best to tell her about everything they saw. But after they passed all of the farms and had been rumbling along a good while, Tinka went silent. She thought this was taking so long. They were going to be driving all day, and there was nothing to see. Uncle Manfred didn't say anything. But when she started to nod, as if she were about to fall asleep, he stopped the cart.

Tinka woke up suddenly when her uncle jumped down over the side of the cart and started cutting pieces of heather with his folding knife.

"What are you doing?" she asked perplexed.

"You might as well lie down and rest, since I know this part of the way," he said, tossing an armful of heather into the back of the cart.

"But I'm not sleepy at all," she said.

He laughed and tossed up some more heather.

"I promise to wake you when I need your help for directions," he said.

Tinka surveyed the landscape. There was a lot of heather and not much else. As far as she could see, everything was brown except for occasional pine trees. It was a dark and desolate area which she must have slept through when she drove through it coming the other way.

"Try this out," said her uncle, tossing one last armful up into the back of the cart.

Tinka crawled down from the bench and settled into the pile of heather, which smelled nice. There were still flowers on some of it. Then Manfred stepped on the hub of the wheel and up and over into the cart again and got the horse moving.

"When we get to a place with decent grass we'll have to stop, so the horse can eat something. And then we can eat too," he said.

When Tinka woke up, he had stopped in just such a place. Manfred loosened the reins so the horse could reach the ground, and he jumped down and started looking for a spring which he thought would be nearby, considering the lushness of the grass. When he found it he led the horse over so it could drink. Then he climbed into the back of the cart with Tinka, and they shared the food they had brought.

When they were finished eating and had drunk at the spring, Manfred thought it was now his turn to take a nap.

"In the meantime you have to make sure the horse doesn't step on soft spots where it can sink in," he said.

Tinka said she would, and her uncle lay down in the back on the heather branches and fell asleep almost immediately. Tinka walked alongside the horse's head and kept an eye out for soft, wet places. The horse grazed eagerly, clouds sailed across the sky, and Uncle Manfred was snoring loudly in the back. Tinka thought they were going terribly slow, and she was feeling impatient, but she didn't dare wake her sleeping uncle. By the time he finally sat up and wiped his eyes, the sun had moved a good distance across the sky.

"Goodness gracious," he said, jumping down and leading the vehicle back to the wheel tracks of the road. Tinka quickly climbed up and sat on the driver's bench. She still didn't recognize any of the scenery, but she hoped she would soon. She sat there looking for the black bog holes which she remembered they drove past on the way out, not long after they passed the area where Larus took the cows to graze.

It was taking longer than she thought, and when she finally saw something gleaming, it wasn't black, but blue. She straightened up in her seat.

"What did you see?" asked her uncle.

"Water, I think. Up ahead. It was very blue."

"Do you recognize it?"

"I don't know yet," she said. "But if it's the bog I'm thinking of, then it won't be much farther to the place where Larus brings the cows."

"So was it somewhere around here you lived with your mother and father?"

"No, that was off to the side. We're not going there. That would take too long." Tinka pointed in the direction where she thought it would be. "There's nothing to see there anyway. The house was burned down."

Then she sat for a long time staring ahead with anticipation, as the body of water slowly glided by. She sat thinking about Larus, and she felt a bit disappointed when they came to the grazing area and it was deserted.

"But at least he was here today," said Uncle Manfred.

"Do you think so?" sighed Tinka.

"Just look there," he laughed, pointing at a fresh pile of cow dung. "That is definitely not from yesterday."

Tinka felt a tug in her stomach at the thought of seeing Larus again. She had thought mostly about Mistress while she was away; but Larus was there too, and he was sad when she left.

After traveling a bit farther they caught sight of Larus walking with his stick behind the cows. The boy turned around when he heard the rumbling of the cart's wheels, and Tinka ducked behind her uncle.

"Crawl back and hide in the heather," he said. "Then you can surprise him."

Tinka did as he said, and Uncle Manfred drove up to Larus, then slowed down to match the speed of the cows. He didn't drive past, even though Larus herded the cows off to the side. It was obvious the boy was feeling uneasy with this strange cart following right behind him, instead of going past in the space he had made. He shouted at the cows to speed up, which made the uncle back off. Manfred didn't mean to hurry the boy or scare him.

But Larus was completely perplexed anyway when this stranger followed him all the way into the farm's courtyard. He was afraid the red-haired man was there to register a complaint about him. But he had made space for him to pass.

Larus entered the barn with the cows so quickly that Mistress sensed something was going on. And then she heard the cart rumble in on the stones.

She walked over to the door and looked out.

She didn't recognize the stranger who had stopped in her courtyard. He wasn't from the village. A sudden fear wound around her throat.

The man on the cart greeted her soberly.

"I have something for you," he said.

Mistress hardly dared to walk over to him. Carefully she looked askance into the back of the cart, where Tinka was lying, her heart leaping in her throat with excitement.

The woman was shocked.

"What happened?" she whispered in dismay.

"Mommy!" shouted Tinka, reaching out her arms.

"Are you alright?" whispered Mistress, still afraid.

"She has just come back home," said the man on the driver's bench. "She's completely fine."

Then Mistress lifted Tinka out of the cart, and tears started streaming down her face. She had to put Tinka down on the ground to wipe her eyes with her apron.

"This is my father's brother," said Tinka, pointing at Manfred. "He drove me home."

"Your father's brother? But it was your mother's parents—"

"They didn't want me after all. They didn't like me. They sent me down to the bog to my father's family."

Mistress shook hands with Manfred and welcomed him.

"We would have liked to have kept her," he said, "but we barely have enough food for ourselves down there."

"Thank you for bringing her," said Mistress. "I won't let anyone take her away ever again."

Then she told Manfred to untie the horse, and she shouted to Larus to open the horse barn and put out some oats.

Manfred protested, but Mistress didn't listen. She instructed him to put the horse inside and to stay at their place for the night.

"But I have to be at work early tomorrow morning," said Manfred. "I only have today for this trip."

"I promise you won't lose out on any wages by not working on Monday," she said.

Meanwhile Tinka had danced her way into the barn to see Larus, who didn't know what to do with himself out of pure shyness and joy. Everything was a big blur to him still.

"I didn't know it was you," he said quietly.

Tinka was beaming.

At the supper table, Master was unusually quiet. He just sat there listening to what Tinka and the stranger had to say. But after the meal he cleared his throat.

"So I guess you would like to have the money to bring back with you," he said to Manfred.

"What money?" said Tinka's uncle.

"The money I got them to pay for having her here all that time. For room and board."

Tinka's uncle shrugged. "They don't know she's back here," he said. "They just came and dropped her off with us. It was the Enegård farmer himself who brought her. If he wants the money back, I guess he'll have to come get it himself."

Master nodded satisfied to himself. It was still a pretty good deal. After they had risen from the table he went outside to dig up some potatoes.

Early the next morning, when Manfred was about to leave, Mistress came dragging an empty wooden basin which she placed up in the cart just behind the driver's bench, after pushing the heather to one side. Manfred watched questioningly, but didn't say anything. The answer came shortly as she began carrying salted meat out in pails from the large tub in their pantry. She brought more and more until the basin was full, then she brought out brine to pour over it. Finally she put the lid on and spread the heather on top.

"Now drive carefully," she told him.

Manfred thanked her, and assured her that there would be a lot of joy in the bog settlement when he came home with this load.

Then Master came over with a large sack of newly dug potatoes, which he flipped up into the back of the cart.

"Something to have with the meat," he said.

Tinka came outside sleep-drunk, and not yet dressed, to say goodbye to her Uncle Manfred. She stood next to Mistress and watched him drive away. Happy to be back, Tinka slipped her hand into Mistress's. This was where she belonged.

In an earnest voice Tinka asked, "Can Larus come back and work here again next year?"

Cecil Bødker (1927-2020) is one of contemporary Denmark's most highly awarded and prolific female authors. She has written 59 books including poetry, novels for children and adults, short stories and plays. Her *Stories about Tacit,* a collection of 11 connected short stories, was published in 1971, forming the first book of The Water Farm trilogy. Best known for her young-adult fiction books, in 1976 she received the international Hans Christian Andersen Medal for Writing for her lasting contribution to children's literature. In 1998 she was awarded the Grand Prize of the Danish Academy for her body of work as a writer.

Michael Favala Goldman (b.1966), besides being a widely-published translator of Danish literature, is a poet, educator, and jazz clarinetist. Over 140 of Goldman's translations and poems have appeared in dozens of literary journals such as *The Harvard Review* and *The Columbia Journal.* He teaches workshops and gives readings at universities and literary events. His fifteen translated books include works by Knud Sørensen, Tove Ditlevsen, Suzanne Brøgger, Knud Sønderby, Marianne Koluda Hansen and Benny Andersen. www.hammerandhorn.net